Frank Walsh's Kitchen and other stories

THE STORY PROJECT OF FILLMORE COUNTY, MINNESOTA

EDITED BY BONNIE FLAIG PRINSEN

NINE DRAGON PRESS
PRESTON, MINNESOTA

www.fillmorecountyjournal.com

International Standard Book Number 0-9746633-1-X

Printed in Canada.

Contents

REMINISCENCE

FOOD

CHARACTERS

LIFE'S LESSONS

Introduction

Editing this collection of stories by Fillmore County residents, the second book of the Story Project, coincided with my taking a class in Native American literature where I became interested in the ways indigenous people use stories to connect with their own history, and how positioning one's self in relation to a *place* is the way history is made.

This concept is not unfamiliar to the people of Fillmore County, where a close connection to the land, in one way or another, has long been a fundamental part of life. I see the writers in *Frank Walsh's Kitchen and other stories* as using stories to position themselves in relation to this place, and thus connecting to history: their own, their families', and the collective history of Fillmore County.

Thank you to Nine Dragon Press for giving me the opportunity to edit another collection of stories. Also, a book like this is not possible without the willingness of local people to put their stories down in writing and submit them, in an act that requires not only time and effort, but a bit of courage as well. And thanks to my mom for her unwavering support of her children's endeavors, and for her encouragement to work hard and do something well, if you're going to do it at all.

Bonnie Flaig Prinsen
Oct. 1, 2005

Choosing this Place

The round barn at JoAnne Agrimson's farm.

"A View of the Prairie"
PAGE 23

*Place has always nursed, nourished and
instructed man; he in return can rule it
and ruin it, take it and lose it,
suffer if he is exiled from it, and after
living on it he goes to it in his grave.*

~ Eudora Welty

The Big Woods[*]

By Dana Gardner

** For locals, "the Big Woods" generally refers to an area near
Canton. But the area north of Lanesboro in the story below is also
known as the Big Woods.*

Many years ago, when I was a teenager, I enjoyed tramping around in a large, wooded area North of Lanesboro, locally known as the Big Woods. I watched birds, hunted for ginseng, looked for spring wildflowers, caught snakes and shiny green tiger beetles, and watched for the early spring arrival of wood ducks on the Root River. In the remote, lower fields bordering the river was a deserted home site. The house was already long gone, and the crumbling remains of a small barn were the only reminder of the homesteaders who had tried to eke a living from the rocky bottomland fields. One spring I poked my head up into the collapsing hay mow to be surprised by two grotesque, fuzzy white, black faced creatures that greeted me by disgorging the smelly contents of their stomachs. A turkey vulture, a rare bird in those days, had chosen the secluded barn to make its nest, and its chicks were not expecting a visitor.

This Big Woods is near the public canoe launch at the Moen Bridge on County Road 8. One enters the woods by driving down a short, dead end, minimum maintenance road that passes by a farm owned at that time by Jake Schaeffer. I waved to him if I saw him outside as I drove by. One early spring day Jake was in his yard when I drove my mom's green Buick, an old car that resembled a heavy armored tank, into the woods. I noticed the rutted road, only recently thawed, was soft and muddy. I decided to turn around rather than risk getting stuck, but turning around on the narrow road was no easy task, and of course I was soon hopelessly stuck. My only choice was to walk out and ask Jake Schaeffer to pull me out with his tractor. He was still out in his yard as I plodded up the hill, as if he were expecting me. "I figured I might as well wait out here," he sternly said, "Cuz I knew you'd be comin' up to ask me to pull you out!" His admonishment made me squirm in embarrassment, but his gruff demeanor belied a soft heart, as he would hear nothing of any payment I offered for his time and trouble.

I grew up and moved away, and a few years later, I wrote to my parents and suggested they take a walk out in the Big Woods and see if the collapsing barn and vultures were still around. They stopped to greet ol' Jake Schaeffer, and ask his permission to walk down to the river. "Sure," he said, "Go ahead. Nobody goes down there anymore, not since that Gardner boy used to tramp around down there." They didn't mention that they knew that Gardner boy.

Now all traces of the homestead have disappeared. Perhaps ginseng is a bit rarer, but turkey vultures are common sights. Plenty of birds and animals still frequent the woods, wildflowers still bloom, snakes and shiny green tiger beetles still scoot across the road, wood ducks fly up and down the river. Much of the land has been bought up by Geoff and Monica Griffin and is a sanctuary for wild creatures. Some of the cultivated land adjoining the woods has been planted into native prairie plants, and the area remains as beautiful as ever. ✽

This Place[*]

By Nancy Overcott

* *The area described in the story below is known to locals as the Big Woods, although other areas, such as the one in the previous story, go by the same name.*

One day last fall, I walked deep into my woods where I hadn't walked in two years and where the trails my husband and I created two decades before hadn't been maintained since I hurt my back in '98. I took a wrong turn and that made all the difference in how I saw the woods. Things had changed of course. The prickly ash, which we had so carefully trimmed, reached across paths tearing at my clothes and skin. The deer and other creatures that helped maintain our trails, had created new ones to detour around fallen trees, thus making me more disoriented than I might have been.

I passed some giant sugar maples that looked like old friends, but they seemed to be in the wrong places. A red-bellied woodpecker called, making me feel at home in spite of being lost. I arrived at one of the benches we had placed along our paths. It wasn't where I expected it to be. My brain tried to make it right and failed. Wasn't this where I used to see a winter wren foraging among the roots of a white oak?

Although I didn't know where I had gone wrong, it soon became obvious that I was going down toward the South Fork of the Root River instead of up to our southern fence-line as I had intended. So I gave up on the paths and headed in the opposite direction. Goldenrod seeds in a brushy area fell off onto my clothes as I pushed through. A chipmunk, with bulging pouches, scurried by. Another startled me with its alarm call. I heard robins and thought maybe they were at the place where I had once found them calling maniacally, flying erratically, and falling off perches, drunk on fermenting cedar berries.

I saw the big oaks as if for the first time and the black cherry trees were larger and more numerous than I remembered. Finally, I reached an old gnarly maple, a friend that was unmistakable due to a branch we had cut for firewood and later regretted. I put my arms around the tree as far as they would go, then felt embarrassed by my sentiment.

About fifty yards away on the other side of our fence line was a field I used to walk across to reach an old tractor path from which I could go down to the South Fork or stay high in the bluffs amidst some towering white pines. On the high route, I would crawl out to a slender point overlooking the creek. From there I could watch fishermen casting their lines for trout and look across the valley to the old Simley farm and what is now the Hvoslef Wildlife Management Area. Once, I watched a red-tailed hawk feeding her young in a nest just below my perch.

As I approached the field, I saw a cabin where no building had ever been. I circled it timidly, like a wild animal, feeling the urge to sniff for danger. No one appeared to be there, so I cautiously stepped onto the porch and looked in a window. I had to shade my eyes because the sun was reflecting the field making it difficult to see inside. The cabin was empty except for something lying on the floor. I caught my breath when I saw the long bill of what looked like a dead woodcock. When I went to the back of the cabin and looked in another window, I realized the woodcock was a toy.

I returned home the way I had intended to come. Everything drew into focus. I finally reached the bench I had been looking for and stopped to rest there, remembering the deer and her fawn that had come within touching distance at this place. The deer weren't there, but, sure enough, a winter wren was foraging among the roots of the oak.

I realized that I have a history in this place and can look back on it almost like I can look back on the town where I grew up. The difference is that I feel I belong here in the Big Woods of Fillmore County, more than I ever belonged in my hometown.

After that day last fall, I walked deep into the woods several more times, trying without success to lose my way. ❈

A Sense of Place

BY BECKY STOCKER

All of us have places in our lives that become special to us. For me, one of those places is a farm just north of Peterson in Fillmore County, Minnesota. Unusual, considering that I grew up about 1,500 miles away from there. Yet each summer we would pack up the station wagon and drive those many miles out to Grandma and Grandpa's farm. The hours went by slowly (especially crossing never-ending Montana) but we would eventually reach Highway 30 where we would pass North Prairie and Arendahl churches, then zoom over the "tickle hills" that left us feeling like our stomachs were bouncing. Only a couple minutes later and we would be piling out of the car, hugging our grandparents, uncles, aunts, and cousins.

I suppose one reason why I loved the farm was because it was so different from where I spent the rest of my life. We lived in the middle of a neighborhood in a large town out West with dry heat and few mosquitoes. No relatives for hundreds of miles. The farm was out in the middle of nowhere with all sorts of room to roam. It was usually hot and sticky with flies and mosquitoes and ticks. And smelly! Everyone could tell if we had spent the morning with the cows or pigs. It was here that I learned the country is not quiet. The birds would wake me in the morning, and frogs would croak me to sleep while the fan hummed along to cool us in the old, old farmhouse without air conditioning.

But the real reason I loved the farm was the people. Even with all the leaves added to the dining room table, there wasn't any room to spare when we sat down to eat, three different generations of our family gathered together. Only after praying "Come, Lord Jesus" would we start passing the platters and bowls and filling our plates. Going into town or heading to church was just like being at a small family reunion! We couldn't go anywhere without running into someone who was somehow related to us. The farm was a place to hear the stories of our grandparents and great-grandparents. Coming to the farm always reminded me that I was connected—to a place, to people, to history, and to God.

Our summer trips to the farm gave me much more than a chance to travel and see a "place." Our trips to Fillmore County gave me a sense of my place in life. Here I was surrounded by those who loved me no matter what and who were happy to enjoy the simple things of life. I was finally able to move to the farm this past fall, and I can't tell you how good it feels to finally be home. ❊

In Less Than an Hour

BY P.J. THOMPSON

The numbers on the clock face glowed red in the darkness. Just the same, I rubbed my eyes to refocus on the digits. "8:30 a.m.—no way!" I said.

Daryl rolled over and affirmed the same time on his wristwatch. "That's what mine says, too. It's because of the rain. I heard we might get a little wet today," he said. He pulled the curtains back from the window and peeked behind the shade. "Maybe even more than a little."

It was the first weekend in September but the weather wasn't exactly cooperating. This was to be our three-day getaway of outdoor sun and fun at our favorite camping spot in Cushon's Peak Campground. The fall usually offers the best camping weather because the bugs are gone and the daytime hours are warm but not too hot. Nights seem darker and sparkle with stars and there's a crisp bite to the air. Sitting around the campfire makes you wish sometimes you were a beast on a skewer that could turn and turn to warm all sides. But there would be little outdoors time today, and even if things let up, the rain-soaked campfire would be tough to start.

After some breakfast, we sipped our coffee and decided it would be a great opportunity to settle in and listen to some music. I grabbed a Patricia Cornwell novel and Daryl plucked out some tunes on his mandolin. Every now and then we'd break into song trying to drown out the sound of the rain outside. Minutes turned to hours and we snacked a little on some fruit and decided to work some word puzzles to activate our brains. Three crossword challenges filled another hour, and the cozy space began to close in by the end of the morning.

"How about a garage sale?" I said. "Let's drive into Rushford and dodge the raindrops. This camper is getting smaller by the minute."

"My back is a bit on the stiff side," said Daryl. "I suppose a drive around the valley is a good way to get out and about. Grab my raincoat there and let's go!"

"Come on, Fudge!" I called to our little pup laying all curled up on the corner of the couch. "We're going for a ride." Bounding off the couch, she went to the door and squealed with delight. I guess it was getting a little too close inside for her as well.

Our tennis shoes squished through the puddles beyond the deck and we reached the cab laughing at one another. It wasn't raining, it was absolutely pouring!

In a short amount of time we reached the edge of the city and slowed the truck to a crawl. There certainly wouldn't be much traffic in this weather and who knew what bargains we'd scout out. We turned down street after street hoping to spy signs or at least some rain-soaked balloons on this September Saturday. The houses on Maple Street all looked like nobody was home. We turned onto Fairy Street and a few garage doors were opened but yawned like empty mouths as cars pulled away for a morning errand. By the time we rolled up Elm and over to Stevens Avenue, the rain had almost stopped. Some children waved from their driveways as they splashed through puddles and picked up worms. "What a quaint little town," I said. "Let's stop at one of those shops we saw when we drove in on the highway. Maybe we can have a sandwich."

Daryl spun the truck around and we passed a lefse shop, a hardware store, a pharmacy and lots of other businesses downtown. "What a neat place with so much to offer," he said. "Maybe we can try north of town before we have lunch. There might be some garage sales there."

Heading north on Highway 43, we went by the high school where teens were playing basketball on the courts in front. Some were visiting with one another and they smiled or waved as we passed. There was a ball field and a beautiful park. We were so involved in conversation, we forgot to look for signs along the road. Before we knew it, we were heading up the hill and out of town. Just as we passed the implement dealer on the north side, I spied a sign. "There, there's one! See, I knew we'd find one if we looked long enough!" I shouted.

Daryl signaled and moved to the right so we could read the address on the small-posted square. But as we approached it was obvious it was not an advertisement for bargains. HOUSE FOR SALE it read. We both began to laugh.

"Oh well, it's as good a place as any to turn around."

So, we turned onto Hillview Drive and continued on. It looked like this road would turn south back into town. We passed several houses and then came to the house with the matching FOR SALE sign in the front yard. "Wow, what a great house!" Daryl said in awe. He picked up his cell-phone and began to dial.
"What are you doing?" I asked.

"What the heck...let's just see what they're asking for the place. It's a beautiful house and look at the location!"

I began to wonder if the rain had soaked more than just the ground around us. "You can't be serious..."

My words drifted into nothingness as he spoke into the receiver, "Hi, my wife and I are sitting on Hillview Drive looking at this beautiful home with the white deck around the front. Yes. How much is it? Well, we're not really looking for a house, we were out for a drive and...well, I suppose, okay....we're not really doing anything else today in this wet weather...about a half an hour? Umm-hmm, sounds good. Sure."

"What are you doing? What are you talking about?" My questions spilled out like the rain that had fallen earlier. Daryl headed left into the steep driveway and parked the truck in front of the garage.

"The realtor just listed it and would like to show it to someone. We're not doing anything anyway and you always said it would be fun to live closer to work."

I think his spontaneity has always been something that made

me smile. He was right. We really had nothing else to do and it would be fun to see the inside of this house.

I grabbed our puppy and jumped down off the running board. There was a garden with an array of pungent flowers. The smell was intoxicating. We looked up the hill as far as we could see through the trees. Oak, birch, pine and butternut trees blanketed the landscape. "I wonder how they mow this place," I whispered as I watched birds of a dozen varieties flit from limb to limb.

"Look at this view!" Daryl was standing at the edge of the driveway now. I walked up next to him to take in the lush picture of the bluffs wrapping their arms around this valley. It was deep green as far as the eye could see and the rain had made everything glisten and smell so clean. The sun started to crawl from behind some clouds and a rainbow formed over the cornfield just down the hill. Caught up in the beauty of everything around us, we hardly noticed the realtor driving in.

"Hey, folks. How are you today? It looks like the sun might just come out!" she said. "I'm Jo and the owner is home and said it's fine to come for a visit right now." We hesitated a moment and she urged, "Oh come on in, it'll be fun. You never know what you might find."

We accompanied her into the house. The smell of fresh baked pie wafted toward us and the owner giggled shyly, "They always say, bake something fresh…but, that's for the church."

Our minds were taking in every corner and every detail. It was perfect and in many ways similar to the house we designed and built back in Maple Lake. The layout was both open and spacious. The airy light-filled rooms left us wondering how we could have stumbled upon such a find. We drifted, almost dazed, from room to room. I had just poked my head into a spacious closet and the realtor rounded the corner. "Well, what do you think?"

"I think we'd like to talk about it for a moment," Daryl said. She nodded and graciously said, "Take your time."

"Let's buy it!" he said. He walked over and turned me around to face the corner room. "This would be a perfect office for you and just think, you'd only have about a half hour drive to work.

I'm serious, I think we should make an offer."

"I can't believe I'm saying it—but, I think you're right. It's exactly what we've been looking for, but I can't wrap my brain around the idea of packing up the house, selling the rental, selling the airplane hangar and selling the business."

"Faith, my dear. It just feels right—don't you think it feels right?"

To this day I'm not sure how we got from the lower level to the dining room table, but we did. We sat down, read the papers, shook hands and bought ourselves a brand new home...in a little less than an hour, with a lot of faith and a gut feeling that seemed to say, "This is where you belong."

Who could have guessed this small village nestled amidst the bluffs of southern Minnesota would one day be called home? It is sometimes difficult to explain to friends and neighbors that it all happened in less than an hour. But, it just goes to show you—home is where you know you belong. We felt it from the moment we walked in the door. ✳

Here on the Beach

By Wayne Pike

If my remarkable memory serves me, I seem to recall hearing that Rugby, North Dakota, is the geographic center of North America. This means that we live just about as far from an ocean beach as we can get. Or, as I am about to explain, maybe we are not that far from the beach.

My family and I recently took a trip to the Pacific Ocean. We walked along the beach and noticed people with long sticks that they jammed into the sand every few feet. They were clam-diggers looking for buried clams. They poked the beach near small bumps in the sand that might indicate the presence of a clam. If the bump was a clam it would reveal itself by moving. When the clam moved the clam-digger would fall upon it with a shovel to dig it up. The digger has to move fast as clams can move through the water-soaked sand at speeds up to an inch per second. In ten seconds they can bury themselves beyond the range of the casual clam-digger's shoveling endurance. Until we talked to these people to find out what they were doing, we were completely unaware of the seafood we were walking on.

We are sometimes unaware of what goes on close to home as well. For example, when I was a kid one of my jobs was to get the cows in from the creek pasture for milking. I often noticed small piles of smooth mud beside golfball-sized holes in the ground bordering the sloughs and swamps. I thought that these mud piles resulted from some activity of a raccoon or snake. I did not know and gave it little thought until years later when I saw these piles again on the edge of a Fillmore County farmer's corn field.

I pointed them out to him and he told me that crayfish dig and live in holes like that. I was doubtful because I had only seen crayfish swimming in creeks. I expressed my disbelief, but the farmer insisted. He said that if I was to dig at that very moment, at that very spot, I would find a crayfish within two feet of the soil surface. This crayfish might even be large enough to eat if I was so inclined to take my seafood from the muddy water on the edge of a cornfield. I was forced to accept him at his word, still wary that my leg was being pulled.

The next afternoon was severely hot and humid, but I felt I had something to prove. I found my trusty spade, rounded up my wife and our three sons, and set out with them to dig up whatever creature lurked in the bottom of that hole. To accentuate their surprise and to minimize my foolishness if it should come to that, I did not tell them what our expedition was all about.

We had to walk about half a mile from our car to the field. I began digging. The first foot or two of soil moved quickly and easily. I expected to see the crayfish crawling out toward me with every shovelful. I continued digging past the three foot level. This crayfish was deep and I had seen no sign of him. The family was getting a bit crabby from standing out in a field on a hot day watching me. They could have done this at home. Finally, the bottom of the hole reached the water table. I cleared away a bit more soil and there we could see the very top of the creature's wriggling antennae. The kids still did not know what it was. I told them I would bring it out for them and leaned far over into the hole. I reached down and, just to make sure there was a little drama, screamed in mock agony while pretending to be jerked farther into the hole. The kids jumped in momentary panic, then laughed at the prospect of having a father who lost a finger to some animal in a hole. The joke turned out to be on me because the crayfish used that opportunity to go to the very bottom of his hole. I had to dig another foot to finally get him out.

We studied the crayfish for quite a while. Each boy got to hold him. It is a family tradition to name every animal that crosses our path so there was a brief debate over an appropriate name for our new pet. We chose Carl as a good name for a crayfish. Then we set Carl free out in the creek in true catch and release style. He was far too small to eat and getting enough more like him to make a meal would have required an army of sore-backed crayfish-diggers like me.

This makes me think of our supposedly solid ground a little differently. Our continent is nothing but a big island. We survive because the ocean is all around and even under us. It is a wonder-filled world we live on. ❋

A View of the Prairie

By Jo Anne Agrimson

When my husband and I moved from our mobile home to our farmhouse eight—can it be eight?—years ago, I removed the huge draperies that had dressed the picture windows in three of our rooms downstairs and took down the yards of sheer curtains that had served as the draperies' undergarments. Only then could we drink in our million-dollar views.

To the south stands the round barn. I hesitate to call it ours, for its existence is a tribute to the ingenuity of Mr. G. G. Gilbertson and its care only recently came into our hands. Framed by fields, the white barn guards our farm, taking up over half of this window.

Here I watch small, rectangular bales of hay squeak their way from the high-sided racks where they have been tossed by the baler, pell-mell, eight or nine bales high at times, to the roof of the barn. The end of a load cues me just as it has cued farm wives for years: when the last bale makes its journey, lemonade and cookies prepare the laborers for another load. Wagon upon wagon, first crop, second crop, and—hopefully—third crop bales lie inside, piled according to value in a code known only to my husband and his brother.

From this window, I view the passing of the farm's seasons as, one by one, the planter, the sprayer, the baler, the swather, the combine, the chisel plow, and, finally, the tractor with its snow blower, parade by, year upon year.

Here, too, the luxury of summer allows me to wave a prayer to my husband as he rumbles off in the '71 Pontiac to do chores on the other farm, both in the morning and after dinner.

To the east, another picture window holds a pasture with its dry run, wandering lazily, wending its way toward some invisible end. Whether peppered by beef cattle or salted with snow, the pasture is crowned by the windbreak of a distant neighbor's farm. Here, the first rays of the rising sun shine between the old maples into our home through the beveled stained-glass window atop the picture window. Each morning, sunbeams create tiny prisms that dance over the floors and walls.

This window captures the arrival of guests as well as their departure. More importantly, as our daughter leaves this home to go to her apartment, we follow a ritual born of our good-byes at her granny's. Stephanie drives ever-so-slowly at first, allowing enough time for us to begin our farewell waves and blown kisses in the south window and finish them at this east window where we wave and wave until her car has completely passed out of sight.

If we had needed a realtor to convince us to purchase this home, either of these views would have sufficed and the deal would have been done. But the final picture window outshines the others.

Minnesota's north winds have prompted some builders to give up completely on any kind of northern exposure to our winters' cruelest weather. No such rule restrained the builders here. They took Genesis literally when they read, "Let there be light," and allowed the north to shine through this home. What was once a formal dining room has become an expanded kitchen, allowing me to keep an eye on the bird feeders and the over-sized back yard that serves its duty as a canvas for any whimsical array of flowers or trees or decorations that seize us at the moment—or as time allows. Although I am the catalyst, my husband wields the shovel ever since my wrists grew prematurely old from one too many nights spent crow-barring the lath and plaster walls that blocked these views.

The northern panorama includes too-few small flower beds; the same wrists that have difficulty making the motions a spade requires would need the same motion to pull weeds. Just as the

farm machinery keeps time on the south side, these few flowers remind us that spring and summer last only a moment. The
seasons pass, from Bleeding Heart to Siberian Iris to Poppies to
Russian Sage. Our trees and shrubs tell time, too, as first one, then
another lilac chooses to bloom, the cherry and the flowering crab
bloom and bear fruit. Now, just beyond the mounds of hydrangea,
the Haralreds decorate the apple tree. How can I bear to pick
them? Though they bend the boughs to their breaking point, and
the breeze teases me with the promise that it can and will make
those apples drop, their harvest can wait.

Beyond them, a barren hay field begins its third effort, and
the fields of corn sandwiching it begin their next stage, denting.
Gazing out, I spy our old tabby cat sneaking a drink of water from
the bird bath as the mourning doves and finches, unperturbed,
continue to feast. Butterflies play tag near the Russian sage. My
to-do list still grows, dishes lie dirty in the sink, and my lesson
plans need a tune-up; but today, just for a few stolen moments, my
window wins. I fetch the half cup of coffee left in the pot and take
a stroll through the yard once more, before this season passes. ✳

Beautiful Mountain

BY JOHN TORGRIMSON

My first glimpse of our farm occurred in June 1994, when our family returned to what the Chinese call America, Beautiful Mountain.

Our farm is small, purchased via a fax machine in Hong Kong through a satellite in outer space to a phone line in Preston, Minnesota. Twenty acres and the buildings and a hundred year old house owned successively by a handful of Norwegians with names like Larson and Kulsrud. Over time, the land was sold off to adjoining farms to make bigger operations with less people working the land. The homestead is what remains.

The pasture is a few yards from the back door. The ground dips where the milk cows worked the fence lines, leaning through the barbed wire for those tender cuts of grass. The beasts worked from west to east, downhill, to the woods where dusk slowly creeps above the hill line toward the valley.

Here the sun follows its daily ritual to rise, in consecutive timelines in Asia and on across countless civilizations, cultures and languages, in the dawn mist on this place in Fillmore County, Minnesota, United States. A very small piece of Beautiful Mountain belongs to us.

There is a granary, hog house, farrowing shed, pole barn, corn crib, summer kitchen and barn. Cast off machinery, boards, wire, chains, and fencing are piled near the buildings, their purposes long forgotten. The barn is a classic piece of prairie architecture, post and beam with mortised columns rising skyward. Hay was hauled into the top floor and thrown down to the waiting animals.

The land lies off of the not so distant prairie, where the glaciers stretched their arms and sent rivulets of runoff on a descending pilgrimage to the Mississippi River. It carved the valleys and arroyos and filled the cracks with creeks and streams. At the top of our wooded hill you can smell the wind from the Rocky Mountains as it crosses from Montana to the plains of North Dakota and Minnesota.

On that first June day, the grass grew knee-high, wild roses bloomed and the neighbor's oats glistened like green velvet in the distance. After Hong Kong, the song of birds in the morning was deafening, the discord replacing the blare of traffic noise on Waterloo Road in Kowloon. My daughter, a child of skyscrapers, concrete and subways, ran barefoot through the grass.

You can walk around the entire farm in a half-hour if you are purposeful about it. The basswoods, elms, walnuts, maples and occasional apple tree line the hillsides and people the pasture. The fencing is haphazard and unlikely to confine anything for very long. And a lonely windmill stands vigil over the valley.

I wonder what China man came up with the name Beautiful Mountain. Perhaps it was an illiterate peasant from Canton who bought his conscription here on a twenty year payment plan to toil under the 19th century sun and steel of the railroads, leaving a wife and children behind in China. Maybe he hired a letter writer in Chinatown that took liberty with the truth, embellishing the possible rather than concentrating on the hardships and privations and the grim realities of time, place and distance. A man child of the diaspora, a victim of literary license.

I think a mandarin, schooled in the classics, thought of Beautiful Mountain. Mountains are a significant theme in Chinese lore and culture. How many paintings focus on mountains? Look at the karst hills of Guillin, captured in ink ground in a stone well and splayed on silk paper. How many poems talk about exile in a misty temple on a lonely mountain like the Tang Dynasty poet, Wang Wei in the "Deer Enclosure"?

On the bare mountain
I meet no one
I only hear the echo of human voices,
Sunlight flickers through the dense wood
And shines full upon the green moss.

For a peasant, a mountain speaks of release from the drudgery of this life. For a monk, a mountain bears witness to pure thoughts of prayers to the hereafter. And for a mandarin, the mountain symbolizes the fulfillment of harmony, that all is perfect in the universe.

After seven years abroad, we came home to Beautiful Mountain, to a farm on the edge of a sea of grass. When times are good, the Chinese say: "The heavens are high and the emperor is far away."

And so they are. ✳

Small Towns

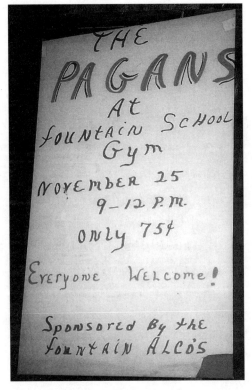

A hand-made poster announces the appearance of
The Pagans at the Fountain High School gym,
November 25, 1964.

*"A Sign of the Times: A Bit of Fountain's
History on Display"*
PAGE 35

*"When Miss Emily Grierson died, our whole
town went to her funeral: the men through
a sort of respectful affection for a fallen
monument, the women mostly out of curiosity
to see the inside of her house..."*

~ William Faulkner, "A Rose for Emily"

Village Lottery

BY DONOVAN RUESINK

As the summertime sun settles into the western sky, the following story-time scene unfolds. It was a Saturday night, complete with entertainment and a cash drawing at the Jack Sprat grocery store. The year was 1939, village of Cherry Grove.

On a homemade platform, local farmers Ray and Allie Lawrence usually were the main attraction. Ray played the harmonica and Allie, the banjo, while as many as fifty to one hundred residents would gather to listen as familiar old American tunes filled the air.

One such local resident was an indigent recluse by the name of Hans Metzer. His home, just two miles south of the village, was a weather-beaten two-story structure with all of the second-story windows broken out. Living there winter and summer, local word was he slept between two mattresses, ate his fried eggs directly from the frying pan, and wore the only clothes he owned. His worldly possessions were a team of horses, a buggy, and a few stolen chickens. Hans too, was attracted to the cash giveaway. Having previously been to the store to purchase five cents worth of candy, Hans watched the storekeeper write his name on a ticket and toss it into the cardboard box. Shortly before the event, people were scattered across Main Street, moving only to let the occasional car venture through. Everyone gathered would also expect Hans's team and buggy to appear from the nighttime darkness. The horses were hitched to the School District 184 flagpole, and Hans would sidle up to the crowd.

This would be the time the local children would spring into action. Sitting straddled on top of the Burrell Crandall stone corner post and pipe rail lawn fence, deathly afraid, all eyes were on the mysterious Hans and his whereabouts. Any glance both real and imagined would send them running into darkness, only to return and repeat the action.

At exactly nine thirty, the storekeeper would appear on the platform, thrash the tickets around in the box, and a local child was chosen to draw two tickets. As soon as the winners of the two-dollar and five-dollar prizes were found to be present, the crowd and Hans himself quickly disappeared into the countryside, only to return hence two weeks in the future.

The storekeeper had achieved his goal of increased business, the residents had participated in a community event, and the indigent went home to ponder. ❋

A Sign of the Times

BY STEVE BEFORT

A piece of local history is on display at the Minnesota History Museum in St. Paul. The historical artifact is a hand-lettered sign advertising a teen dance in the Fountain elementary school gym during the 1960's.

The sign is part of the museum's "Sounds Good To Me" exhibit honoring Minnesota's musical history. The exhibit features Minnesota artists and music venues. The exhibit includes interactive displays in which visitors can select jukebox hits in a cafe setting that spans multiple decades or sing along with the 1980 Minnesota-produced hit "Funkytown."

The Fountain sign announces the appearance of a rock band called "The Pagans" at the Fountain school gym on November 25. While the sign does not note the year, it most likely was 1963 or 1964. The entry fee was 75 cents. The dance was sponsored by the "Fountain Alco's." The sign itself was donated to the museum by ex-Pagan Kip Sullivan of Rochester.

The Minnesota History Center likely displayed this sign to depict the proliferation of garage bands during the 1960's as well as the grass roots nature of entertainment during that era in small-town Minnesota. But, if this sign could talk, it would tell a far richer story.

The Fountain Alco's, or all-community volunteers, grew out of the desire of a handful of Fountain teens to bring some entertainment to a town of 300 people that rolled up its streets at the end of the work day. The teen group initially rented the town's elementary school gym for a dance featuring a portable record player. The group gambled that a 25 cents entry charge would cover the five dollar gym rental fee. When that venture proved profitable, the teens began to book local bands such as Lanesboro's Trashbeaters at somewhat higher stakes. Continued success led to better known acts, including regional headliners such as The Pagans and The Mustangs from Rochester.

Rita Rustad was the idea person behind the dances. I booked the bands and worried about the organizational details. And a whole host of our friends contributed to make the events happen. Not the least of these contributors were the sign makers, such as Terrie Rustad, Linda Asleson, and Nancy Stevens. Their signs appeared all over Fillmore County during dance season.

The financial success of the dances presented a dilemma of sorts—what to do with the profits? The teen group eventually decided on an all-community solution. For several years, the dance proceeds financed free bus trips to the Minnesota State Fair in St. Paul for all Fountain-area teenagers. About forty teens would depart from the Fountain post office at 6:00 a.m. and begin the return trip only after the end of the fair's grandstand act. The day-long marathon at the fair remains a unique memory for many Fountaineers.

The dance sign, in short, reflects a period in which small-town kids scrambled to provide their own entertainment. In addition to the dances, these Fountain teens organized co-ed softball games at the Catholic churchyard, flooded the town skating rink, and created a swimming hole by damming a creek in the Big Springs. In an ironic twist, the old Fountain elementary school where the dances took place now houses the Fillmore County History Museum.

I wish that all of our old gang of Fountain teens could experience the thrill of stumbling upon this sign as I did. But, not all of them are still with us. In particular, sisters Rita and Terrie Rustad, though opposites in many ways, shared the tragic fate of being cut down in the prime of life by breast cancer. This dance is for you. ❋

Happiness at Christmas from Coast to Coast

By Beverly Lewis Crowson

A 1940's Christmas at Coast to Coast Hardware in Chatfield always featured a section of toys, a very large section where other merchandise gave way to the things that a child's dreams were made of. The kids would get the news at the elementary school on Main Street that the toys "are at the store", and everyone would troop in to pick out what they, if they could, would choose as their most perfect gift for Christmas. We were not to touch, and all tried to honor that, just so we could be there in that magical place. But those were the War years, and often there was no connection between dreams and the reality of finances at home. It was a time of doing without.

I remember the Christmas when I was eight years old, walking slowly down the aisle looking at the beautiful dolls, lying so perfectly in their boxes in their satin dresses. I had never had a new doll and certainly nothing like those with their dimpled knees and angel smiles. In the last box on a high shelf near the corner was the biggest baby doll I had ever seen. If I stood on tiptoe, I could see her sweet little face just over the side of the box. From that moment, I loved her with all the yearning of one who supposed it could never be. But the hardware store lay in the homeward path from school so while my sisters looked at other things, I could visit the special aisle and the beautiful baby doll.

One day shortly before Christmas, during one of my visits, I realized the box had been moved and I could see her much better, could see that she had been out of the box and had evidently hit the floor face down, causing a big "hurt" on the side of the forehead. One of the clerks came by and told me the doll had actually been damaged in shipment, and hadn't I seen that there was a problem with this doll? I remember that sometime during that visit I began thinking of a Christmas miracle. Maybe, just maybe, now just a small amount of money could be enough now.

All the way home as I tagged along behind, I kept seeing the little face that had something wrong with it, and the doll seemed to become truly mine as I thought about my own face and my eyes and the ugly glasses I had to wear and be called "four eyes" and other names as cruel as the hurt on the baby's face. But at home where there were three other children and no money to spare, the truth came crashing down, and no amount of talking seemed to move my mother who knew the rent, the groceries, fuel oil for the heater and maybe some shoes for Christmas would leave nothing for even the cheapest doll for a heartbroken little girl.

Christmas Eve came, and somehow there were new pajamas under the tree, and we four children put them on and danced around in a circle, happy with the gift and being together. And when I, laughing and falling down next to the tree, saw what was nestled there, I looked at my mother who smiled her beautiful smile and said, "Yes, she is yours."

I never discovered who was responsible for the Christmas miracle. Did my mother, empowered by her love and desire to give to her child, stiff-arm her pride and go for a talk with the owner of the store? Had the clerks weighed in on the side of "the kid who always comes to visit"? Perhaps the owner, who was like so many in small towns during that time of pulling together, said, "Of course, she can have the doll."

I loved the doll beyond words, and learned something more: that Christmas was about love and kindness that exist around and for a child within the circles of family and a small community. ✳

Rollerskating

BY MARCELLE VRIEZE SHIPTON

I lived on a farm behind the Rock Quarry on Rifle Hill Road, County Road 14. The driveway was 3/8 of a mile long and a creek ran through the driveway. When it rained hard, the creek came up and we couldn't get in or out until the water went down and the road was muddy.

I loved to rollerskate and I didn't drive yet, so when I wanted to go rollerskating on Friday night I'd hitch a ride with Neil Heusinkveld. I'd light a lantern and walk out to the road and we went to Greenleafton Hall owned by Bill Prinsen where we skated. Skates cost twenty five cents to rent. The most fun was when Harlan Grooters and a few other skaters behind him would form a line and crack the whip. I loved to be on the end to get a good fast ride. Neil would let me off at the driveway. I'd light the lantern and walk home. I had no fear, even if an owl hooted.

Glenn and I got married April, 1947 and the old driveway was still there. The road was muddy and we couldn't get out with a car. The car was left at the end of the driveway. Dad had to take our clothes and all the things we needed for the wedding out to the road with a team and wagon. It was a chore, but we got married at the Greenleafton Reformed Church, a little while before it was struck by lightening and burned.

Years later a new driveway was made above the creek so we didn't have to worry about rains and mud anymore. ✳

Lost and Found

By Marjorie Taylor Smith

"There he is now."

Citizen Smith stopped by the City Hall to pay a bill. He found the office staff plus the street crew loitering and chuckling over an object they passed around to be examined. One of them came over to him with said object and asked, "Is this yours?" It was "uppers" from a set of false teeth! Everyone in town knew the tale of Smith's lost uppers.

"Naw, I don't think so," said Smith. "—wait a minute. Here is that mark that was on my teeth!" It was indeed, on that March day, the plate Smith had inadvertently flushed away after the town celebration held the past July. A stray virus had sickened Smith and with it had disappeared his teeth down the "john."

The city crew had been flushing mains which have traps here and there; in the one from Smith's area of town these teeth surfaced, having been gone eight months. Now they were found. Needless to say, Smith had long since got a new denture. The cruddy, now famous, historic teeth repose in wax paper, in a box, where you wouldn't want to see them. Or would you? ✳

The Tawney Store

By Gary Stennes

"Are we there yet? Are we there yet? Are we there yet? Hey dad? Are we there yet?"

I'm sure I drove my parents crazy on those long car rides down Highway 43. There were so many corners and hills on that road, and I was just so impatient about getting there. We were going to visit Grandma and Grandpa Stennes at, what seemed to me at the time, a slice of heaven on earth. Grandma and Grandpa owned the Tawney Store.

I just thought it was so neat that there was a store in the front and a house in the back. I probably spent more time in the store than in the house. I remember Grandpa sneaking me candy bars, potato chips and slices of fresh-cut summer sausage.

I loved sitting on the front porch with my snack and just watching the traffic go by or listening to Grandpa shoot the breeze with a customer buying gas.

I also remember finally finding out what that little building with the crescent moon on the door was. Really now, that was the coolest discovery yet! Grandma and Grandpa had a bathroom in the house and one outside of the house! It sure came in handy when we were all hard at play and nature called.

One day my cousin Angie was very excited to inform me that she had found some "toy cigarettes." We put them in our mouths and were playing 'grown up" and boy did we think we were hot stuff. We walked in the house to show our mothers, thinking they would be impressed with our toys, only to have them yank the objects from our mouths in disgust. We were so confused. We later

41

found out that we were sucking on someone's old cigar holders. I feel sick to my stomach just thinking about it.

The old Tawney Store is gone now, as are Grandma and Grandpa. Every time I drive past the marker that takes its place, I think how it's too bad that time can only move forward. A comforting thought, however, is that memories never die. ✻

The Natural World

"Tooey", after his eighteen year imprisonment in
Wayne Pike's freezer.

"Fish Out of Water"
PAGE 50

And did you get what you wanted in this life
even so? I did. And what is it you wanted?
To call myself beloved.
To feel myself beloved on the earth.

~ Raymond Carver

Tornado Watch

By Trudy Schommer

Perhaps it is my lack of experience. Perhaps it is a love of danger and excitement, but I have never been afraid of tornadoes. Yes, I've seen the damage and destruction that they can do, but I also remember the thrill I experienced as a child when the wind blew so strong I could almost lean into it and not fall down as I hurried to bring my father's cattle in from the threatening storm.

So when, as an adult, I came up against a tornado, I did not get terribly frightened. It was in early summer and I was at a camping retreat. Each of us had our own tent and we had settled in for the night. I had just gotten into my sleeping bag when the director of the retreat came to my tent and gave me the news that there was a tornado warning for our area. I asked her what everyone else was going to do and she said, "I think that they are coming to the main building." The main building was the food preparation center, and had the showers and toilet facilities.

I thanked her and then thought to myself, "I won't be any safer there than I am here." And so I hunkered down in my sleeping bag and waited to see what would happen.

It did not take long before the wind began to blow, and I wondered if I had made the right decision. As the wind increased, so did the noise and soon it sounded like a train was going to run over me. I began to fear for my tent and myself.

After a while, however, the wind died down and it began to rain. It continued to rain for quite some time, and soon I heard the call of nature. I thought to myself, "I can't go up to the main building now. They'll just say to me, 'Well, now's a fine time to come!'"

So I took off my pajamas, went out into the rain and just allowed myself to experience the feel of the heavy downpour. I took care of my need and went back into my tent. I dried myself off, climbed back into my sleeping bag, and went to sleep. The only one who saw me in the rain was God, and She said it was "okay!" ❋

Tick Removal

By Jeff Kamm

D o you swat at imaginary things and constantly check the waistband of your underwear after a day in the field?

Do you spray more than one can of DEET on yourself prior to walking across a grassy field or walking through the woods?

Do you stand in front of a full length mirror for twenty-five minutes or more making ridiculous bending movements trying to check your entire body for ticks?

After a day in the field do you shower to the point of chafing because someone in your hunting party found a tick on his dog?

If you answered "yes" to three out of four questions, read on, you might be suffering from "tick distress".

The way Billy was jumping around and yelling at the top of his lungs, I could only figure he had just seen a bear. Billy and I were on a weekend vacation. We were enjoying a little canoeing and camping down the North Branch of the Root River in Southeastern Minnesota. At the time of all this commotion, Billy was about a quarter mile up stream. Billy was working a silver and red spinner back and forth across the Root. Fishing had been great the last few days. Another trout dinner didn't sound half bad. I was down stream lying stretched out in the canoe soaking up a spectacular mid-July sun. As much as I tried to ignore Billy's frantic howls, I could not. Grudgingly, I was going to have to beach the canoe and walk up the river bank and see what all the commotion was about.

Here's the scene: first off Billy is not a small boy. This man played defensive tackle at a Division I University and started all four years. He is 6'5" tall, goes about two seventy, and is still very fit. However, there was no question that Billy was excited, jumping around as if his shorts were on fire and pointing to his forearm. Growing more concerned, I approached apprehensively. "What's the matter?" I asked. Billy pointed to his forearm and there was a wood tick attached to it. "Get it off me, would you!", Billy beseeched. Mind you, I'm not a fan of the wood tick either, but after all, Billy's wife, my sister, would never forgive me if I let him die out here in the wilderness, so I plucked the blood sucker off his arm.

That night sitting around the campfire, I couldn't help but give special attention to every bug that crawled through my hair. Every once in awhile I would shift positions in my camp stool and a blade of grass would inadvertently rub against my bare leg. I would reach down and slap my leg just to make sure it wasn't a tick looking for a place to settle into.

I have had my own disconcerting experience with a wood tick. I was canoeing the Boundary Waters Canoe Area of Northern Minnesota. The fishing group decided to fish some of the remote small lakes in the area, off the beaten path and away from the maddening crowd—wood tick country you might say. To get to these small lakes would require the group to do some portaging through the woods, a small price to pay for an opportunity to fish these pristine lakes. The fishing turned out to be fantastic that day, and the group was well rewarded for the extra effort to get to these fishing honey holes.

Later that evening I decided to take a well deserved bath in the lake, using biodegradable soap, of course. As I stood before Mother Nature, feeling that freedom that only baring yourself in this fashion can bring, one of my fishing buddies looked over and asked "What's the black spot on your butt?" I had a wood tick attached to my rear. I figured I had two problems: first, I was unable to reach the tick myself, and second, how do you ask a buddy to pick a tick off your butt? After some discussion pleading, and overly macho protesting, my friend finally removed the tick.

As Billy and I shoved off the next morning and headed down the Root towards the end-of-the-weekend pick up point, my thoughts were on the weekend events. God bless these little blood sucking misfits. As much as we hate to have ticks on us, tick removal stimulates a whole new mixture of myth, legend, and real truth. We equally hate to have to pull them off. But wood ticks are a reality of spending time in the woods, and, like everything else, can be dealt with. ✻

Fish Out of Water

By Wayne Pike

About a year after we were married, I took my wife out trout fishing for the second time in her life. As luck would have it, she hooked the largest brown trout I had ever seen. It was twenty-two inches long and weighed over four pounds. She wanted to take it home and eat it. I insisted that, because it was the first trout she had ever caught, it should be mounted. We named the trout "Tooey", decided on his gender, placed him in a plastic bag and put him in the freezer to await a trip to the taxidermist.

I did not anticipate that Tooey's wait would be quite as long as it turned out to be. We were farming at the time and we were too busy to get to the taxidermist that summer. Later on, when we had more time, we had even less money. Tooey stayed in the freezer and traveled with us as we moved from place to place seeking a new place to root.

Tooey's frigid plight was always in the back of my mind. About two years after Tooey joined our family, I talked to a taxidermist who was looking for business at a county fair. I was disappointed to learn that a fish kept in the freezer for two years would probably not be a good candidate for mounting. He explained that the skin dries out rapidly in a freezer and would likely be ruined.

Over the ensuing years, Tooey made several trips out of the freezer for exhibitions to privileged friends and neighbors. Otherwise, he got in the way in more ways than one. He took up freezer space and had to be carefully packed around so he would not get his fins broken. He was also a reminder to my wife that she was right and that we should have eaten him the day she caught

50

him and that I was at least partially mistaken for wanting to have him mounted. That is an approximation of her actual words and feelings expressed on several occasions.

Finally, after eighteen years in the freezer, Tooey found himself lying on the workbench in a taxidermy shop. I had sneaked him out of the freezer and was determined to put an end to his state of suspended animation. Either he was getting stuffed or he was going to be cat food.

The taxidermist politely admired him for a minute and then said, "He's been in the freezer a while, I see."

"Yeah. I didn't have the money to have him mounted when we caught him so I put him in the freezer," I told him, hoping that would end this line of questioning.

"How long? A couple years?"

"Oh, yeah. I suppose."

He let me off the hook when he told me that he thought that he could save Tooey. Technology had advanced during the time Tooey had been in the freezer and I had stumbled upon one of the best taxidermists around. I gave him the required down payment and he assured me that Tooey would be mounted and ready for a Christmas delivery.

I gave myself several pats on the back on my way home. My first success was that Tooey had successfully sneaked out of the freezer without being caught again. Secondly, Tooey was in good enough shape to be mounted. And thirdly, here it was only July and I had my wife's Christmas present selected. Like they say, it didn't get any better than this.

I should have known better. The fish in the freezer that had become a thorn in our marital side was suddenly found missing just two days later. So much for surprises. I had to confess that I took her fish, but had not disposed of it. I did not go into detail, but she must have known what was going on. After all, how many things can you do with a fish that has been dead and frozen stiff for eighteen years?

My stuffed fish gambit also failed to relieve my Christmas shopping stress. About a month before Christmas, I started calling the taxidermist to make sure that Tooey would be ready in time. The taxidermist continually stated that he was sure it would be, but he could never remember who I was or what I had brought in to have done. Finally, two days before Christmas, I called and was told that Tooey would be ready that afternoon. To complete the stomach-acid scenario, a freezing rainstorm was moving in.

The kids and I managed to make the pick-up without incident. I breathed a sigh of relief when I saw Tooey in all his stiff and shiny mounted glory. Before we left, I confessed to the taxidermist that Tooey had really been in the freezer for eighteen years, not the two years that he had guessed earlier.

Tooey was certainly not the biggest fish the taxidermist had ever stuffed, but I could tell from the look on his face that I was the biggest procrastinator ever to set foot in his shop. ❄

The Raccoon

By Tom Driscoll

It happened in Amish country up on Oak Hill at the end of the rocky lane, that big old white house looking down at muddy South Fork.

My dogs, from the time I got up that morning, were acting nervous, scrabbling around on the porch to grab three-or-four bits of dry food from a big blue bowl by the kitchen screen door. I poured myself a cup of coffee and filled the work Thermos. My three 40-pound mutts colored jet black, red ale and towhead crunched food, chattered across weathered floorboards, their toenails long from the muddy spring, noisy as children playing with dice. Down the front steps they trouped, and across the yard to an old willow tree splayed by lightning beside the red toolshed.

Overnight chill clinging to unwashed windows already felt warm when I pushed my face against cracked panes to watch my dogs one-at-a-time poke their noses under that shaggy willow, then lurch backward. They each did this a few times before packing back to the porch for more food, loud chewing and the clack-clack of black toenails.

Forgetting the dogs for a minute, I shoved a dark bread sandwich into my wrinkled lunch sack and sipped steaming coffee cooling with the slow certainty that by noon my cheddar cheese slices would soften to the contours of thick-sliced summer sausage. It would be a hot day, good for framing roofs.

Again, I heard the dogs murmuring outside, their heavy ceramic food bowl bumping against an old round porch column. "What?" I finally shouted. Three grinning dogs pushed their rubber noses against the rusting backdoor screen, hips waggling, tails aswing like skipping ropes. "Something botherin' you out there?"

To the east, a cool row of pines separated the uncombed willow from old farmer Joe's plow-blackened soy field grown dusty-green with bean sprouts. Underneath branches spraying gracefully up, then down again, like water from a hose, lay the raccoon.

For a spooky second I feared the dogs had really found a young child, so big was the raccoon, and lying on its back, spread-eagled like that, or a child's broken horse. Then I relaxed, believing it dead, and whistled my dogs to back off, give me space to kneel in red pine needles and worm beneath willow whips still prickly with spring buds.

If dead, it was fresh-dead, the raccoon on the bed of half-frozen humus, sickeningly warm, its blood crimson, its muscles visibly stiffened. The dogs bumped into each other and nipped at the frayed blue pockets of my faded work jeans. Should they dive on the raccoon, they wanted to know, tear it up and toss its parts about like an old chew toy? What should they do? The raccoon excited them. Could they have it? Please?

I slithered close, afraid the dead raccoon might jump me awake, and claw off my nose before ripping out the eyes of the dogs who had first disturbed its slumber. It's big, and surely would be a fierce coon upon a dog were its belly not sliced open. But not shot, that I could tell, lying there on its back begging the question dogs never ask—why? It was still bleeding. Gravity struggled to pull its paws into the ground.

The dogs whimpered and tried to crawl under the tree with me and the raccoon in the winter shade, a south wind draping branches like a damp dishrag. My eyes giant telescopes, I gazed back in time to watch the rabid claws of coonhound ripping through broomthick coonfur, a frantic coonhunter clubbing, kicking to get the raccoon off his dog. Gravely wounded, the raccoon must have made its way through thick timber lining ravines clear down to South Fork to get up here and die under my willow.

Is it alive? Have my dogs not dragged it around the yard while I was making lunch because the raccoon has hissed at them like a snake, swiped at their noses, a compromise to wrastle dogs no more in exchange for not ending up a spilt bag of broken bones in the jaws of dog?

There was no movement of the ribcage, but I felt raccoon breath and laughed nervously like a dog unable to resist poking its nose against the backdoor screen. Supporting myself on one elbow, I tried to touch the back of the black-clawed paw nearest me when suddenly up sat the raccoon, grabbing two of my fingers. The pressure of five steel-sharpened awls eased up just before breaking my skin. Walnut raccoon eyes and its bloody grimace promised to rip out my throat if I moved any closer. I felt hot wind not breath, and the coon stiffened its spine above the belly wound, and its eyes filled with purple ink.

This really impressed my dogs. They moved in close to smell the marvelous conjunction of life and death as the raccoon released my fingers, its beautiful mask relaxed from predator to resemble cartoon again. Menace dissolving at my fingertips, the raccoon sighed, lay back down and yielded to betrayal by dogs.

If it was the size of a rabbit, I think, like the rabbit I killed after the dogs mangled it, I could easily kill it, a soft, warm rabbit under a coarse burlap sack, under my calloused hand, a rabbit no longer afraid of dogs. And smashed the rabbit's skull with a hickory stick two inches thick. And the breath of the rabbit moved up the stick into my muscles, the shimmering final animal pang quickly gone. In a hot fire, in the rusted trash barrel where I had often thrown dead birds and slow squirrels, I burned the burlap sack with the rabbit inside, lavender flames joyfully consuming fur and bone the way teething dogs chew and chew and chew.

So I ran my dogs down to the old keeled-over corncrib and rousted sleeping, straw-colored cats to fetch another burlap sack, and I ran back and tried to cover over the raccoon. Unsure, I knelt under the tree holding a length of galvanized drain pipe. But the raccoon grabbed my sack and pulled me closer. The dogs sprang backward. The raccoon grumbled low, bared its rusted teeth, its tongue a dusty road. Never would it hide under a grass bag while I smashed its head, not while strength remained in its paws to tear off my hand and eat it in front of me, then kill the dogs and eat them too. And let go the sack, and me. And fell back to earth beneath the willow, a deflated flat except for the meager crown of its ribs.

Well I had a big, heavy kettle, which I lugged under the tree and tipped carefully over the raccoon. Off to work I drove knowing my dogs, even if they tried, could not bother the poor beast buried beneath the pot. That day one of the other carpenters showed up at the job with a bale of frozen coonskins that he peeled apart and spread out on a gravel pile to thaw. A fur buyer came by at lunch and paid 900 dollars for the raccoon pelts. Now I already knew from countless lunch hour tales that this carpenter was a diehard coon hunter. I'd seen his hunting outfit, oversized pants and shirt stiff with rancid coongrease, his shotguns, Willie and Waylon, his illegal spotlights. He had three dogs of his own, expensive Bluetick hounds. Turns out, after work the night before, he was out coon hunting along the river when his 1200-dollar coonhound Duke treed a hugely-monstrous coon, and before he could shoot it that coon come down that damn o'cottonwood and commenced to fightin' with o'Duke and looked like o'Duke might even win when that o'coon jumps up and grabs o'Duke by the back of the neck and starts shakin' him so hard o'Duke's ears was flappin' and would have bit clean through the dog's spine except my other two-worthless-one-thousand-and-two-hundred-dollars-coonhounds finally show up and scare that coon away. But didn't even bother to shoot that worthless coon, its fur's all chewed up and ain't no good to nobody now. But don't have no choice but to shoot o'Duke, so tore up he is he ain't worth savin' even.

One muggy end of summer day, my dogs peacefully snoozing on the cool gray planks of the shaded porch, old farmer Joe's beanfield already yellowing, the strawberry-blond willow drooping with thirst, ground underneath brittle as an old tombstone, I lifted the heavy pot to reveal an exact circle of pure black stink, a portrait of raccoon death, its anonymous stain leeching deep into the roots where once the raccoon held me by the claw. ❄

56

A Skunk's Legacy

By Wayne Pike

One late winter evening, our sons came running in from the barn to report that they had seen a skunk dining at the cats' steel feed pan. They encouraged me to get the gun. I found my shotgun and dusted it off. I don't use it very often, and I wasn't sure that blasting away in the barn at night was the best way to get the target practice I needed. Although the shotgun was easy to find, the ammunition was not. The skunk was gone by the time I finally found the dilapidated cardboard box of shotgun shells. I was somewhat relieved.

Several days passed without a skunk sighting and I was thinking that our problem might have solved itself. Then late one evening, when I was already in my jammies, a son came in and said that the skunk was back. I was somewhat more prepared this time. I had found my rifle and ammunition for it. I figured that the rifle would be better for the barn walls if a confrontation with the skunk came down to indoor gunplay. I grabbed two bullets and headed out. Peeking in the barn window, I noticed the cats sitting high on the firewood pile. They were peering down at a hefty skunk eating their food.

I loaded my rifle with my two bullets and, in best TV show fashion, pushed open the barn door to face the skunk. He was already headed for cover. I took careful aim and fired away.

I need to explain that it had been quite a while since I shot my rifle. The last time I used it was outdoors, in the daylight, and aiming at a stationary target. It was also before I started wearing bifocals. Let's just say that the two bullets that I had hastily pulled out of my pajama pocket were not going to be enough.

I beat a hasty retreat back to the house while the skunk forti-fied his position under some debris in the corner. This time I reloaded with a fair degree of serious intent. I cleaned my glasses and practiced kinking my neck so that my eye could find that little bead on the far end of the gun barrel. While doing so, I realized that I had forgotten how tiring it is to run and curse at the same time. When I was good and ready, heart rate down to less than thumping, respiration steady and vocabulary under control, I went back for the next battle.

This time the rascal thought he was hiding and stood still. It only took four or maybe five precisely placed shots to make sure he was dead. I was going to have to move some heavy stuff to get his body out of there, and I wasn't going to do that in my pajamas. It was late and it was starting to smell bad in the barn, so I decided to leave the clean up until the next day. This decision allowed the skunk to leave his legacy.

Unfortunately, our garage is on the opposite end of our pole shed barn. There are two interior walls separating the barn from the garage, but the garage stunk as bad as the barn. Even worse, the cars smelled as bad as the garage. It took about a week for the smell to leave the vehicles.

I was fortunate in this adventure in at least one way. My wife is "nasally challenged" when it comes to smelling a skunk. She described the smell in the barn that almost sickens me as, "a little off-odor when I go right in there." This spared me a week's worth of chastisement for the way I conducted the skunk works. ✻

Ginseng Hunting

BY JOHN TORGRIMSON

In early September when ginseng season starts, I usually spend an afternoon or two walking the hills, especially on a day when a slight wind rustles the trees and the sun filters down from above. The forest floor in late summer gives off a sweaty, musky scent that says that things are either growing or soon to decay.

I first went ginseng hunting over ten years ago when two friends introduced me to the mystical plant. Their attempts to describe to me what ginseng looked like were lost in a sea of green and yellow that filled my vision at every step. And when one of them found a plant and dug the root, I took the plant with its multiple clusters of five leaves around with me, telling myself to find a plant that looks like this.

Initiation to the status of ginseng hunter requires one to find a plant on his own. The problem in hunting ginseng is that you have to be able to focus your mind on the shape of the leaves and the unique clusters so as to mask out the rest of the plant life on the forest floor. It is a kind of walking, thinking, seeing meditation—zen in greens and yellows.

In my second year of seeing ginseng, I found a Buddha Root. Freshly dug, the root stretched from my chin to my belt. It resembled a river system and all of its tributaries and as it dried in my kitchen, it became more and more like a Chinese man growing old with great long wisps of beard sprouting from its chin. The more the root resembles a man, or Buddha, the more value it has in the eyes of Asians.

I gave the Buddha Root to a Chinese friend of mine on the

occasion of her wedding. Years later, I saw a similar, but smaller root for sale in an herbal medicine shop in Hong Kong. Tucked amidst the deer horn and other exotic flora and fauna, the sight of the plant took me back to the hills of Fillmore County. But I soon sobered up when I saw that it was selling for U.S. $1,500.

Renshen, the Chinese word for ginseng is formed by two characters: Man and Root. Thus, ginseng is "the root that looks like a man." There are two basic types of ginseng, that from East Asia (Korea and China) and that from America (Minnesota and Wisconsin). The Chinese believe that American ginseng is "cooling", that it reduces an overheating metabolic rate while at the same time invigorating the system. Korean/Chinese ginseng has the heaty effect of raising the metabolic rate.

Consequently, Chinese prefer American to East Asian ginseng and often prepare it in a chicken broth. A Laotian friend once told me that he puts ginseng in whiskey to drink as a medicine.

These and other thoughts were on my mind a few weeks ago as I made my solitary pilgrimage to the hills. Standing alone in the woods, on a day when summer begins its hesitant decline into autumn, was more than reason enough to be where I was. And while leaves rained all around me and waltzed in the September foliage, my mind became clear, my soul calm. ✳

Close Calls

Carol Thoun in her caving helmet
(with a carbide lamp) during her days as
a guide at Mystery Cave.

"The Day the Lights Went Out at Mystery Cave"
PAGE 79

"Sweet are the uses of adversity"

~ William Shakespeare

Welcome Back

BY LAVERNE C. PAULSON

I was lying on my back in a hospital bed in the cardiac intensive care unit somewhere in St. Mary's Hospital. It was late at night or early morning, but I had no idea what hour it was. My family had gone home earlier and would be back in the morning before my surgery. I could remember only bits and pieces of the last twenty-four hours.

I remember a digital clock reading 11:11 when I woke up on the evening of November 11. I could barely breathe. A hundred knives were going through my chest. Someone was standing on my chest while someone else was trying to rip my left arm from my body.

As an EMT with the Preston Area Ambulance for more than twenty years, I kind of recognized the symptoms, but I was barely fifty-three years old, much too young for a heart attack. I dialed 911 and requested the Preston Ambulance. An excellent ambulance crew, several aspirin, a few nitro, a log of oxygen, a Gold Cross intercept, an IV, and a lot of prayers got me to St. Mary's alive.

Over the years, I had watched countless monitors during hundreds of emergency trips to the ER. Trust me, those same monitors look a lot different when you're the patient hooked up to them. There was something about the peaks and valleys on that EKG that didn't look exactly normal.

At the hospital, Denise would talk to me in a reassuring way between trips to here and there for this test and that. "They are keeping you overnight for observation and perhaps you'll go home in the morning." I wanted to believe her, but deep down I knew it might be longer. After some time, I was assigned a room with a lot of equipment and a nurse who never strayed too far. Neither Denise nor I got a whole lot of sleep that night.

The next morning I was informed I had been scheduled for a somewhat unpleasant angiogram which went off more or less without a hitch, what I remember of it. While I was in recovery, a surgeon whom I would get to know a lot better in the next few days, informed me of blockages of 85 to 95 percent, and neither stents nor balloons were advised. Surgery was the only option. He wasn't sure how extensive. Two, three, four, or five by-pass. I jokingly asked for a second opinion. He said, without any hesitation, "Without this surgery, you won't last three weeks, perhaps not three days."

The surgery would take place the following afternoon.

I was taken back to my room to lie completely still for hours so the incision where the camera had been inserted would heal before my surgery. I had a lot of visitors in the next few hours. Friends and relatives stopped by, chaplains, doctors. The nurse and my family never strayed far. After the ten o'clock news, I told Denise to go home and get some sleep. She'd spent the night before in the ER with me. I knew she'd be back early in the morning to spend some time with me prior to surgery.

The night dragged on. Would morning never come? My nurse stayed very close checking this and that, wondering about pain and if I needed any morphine. The machines I was hooked up to beeped, hissed, and clicked monotonously. They seemed to talk secretly among themselves. They didn't speak my language and I was tiring of them. There was nothing worth watching on TV. I was not experiencing pain, or at least nothing requiring morphine. I assumed the nitro drip was helping with that.

As sleepless hours passed, I had a strange feeling that something was happening. The nurse noticed something suspicious on the monitor and asked me if I was okay. I assured her everything was fine, although that was not exactly truthful. She told me the monitor showed I was experiencing pain, and once again asked me if I wanted morphine. I declined. "If you change your mind," she said, "just push that button to call me and I will be here within seconds."

As she walked from my bed, a great pressure began to build within my chest and that guy was back, standing on my chest. I squeezed the button. She was at my side in a second or two with morphine in hand. "This will help," she assured.

It didn't. The pain worsened. She glanced at a monitor and I heard her exclaim to someone near by, "Blood pressure is sixty and falling!" That was the last thing I remember hearing.

Yellow-red-orange. Yellow-red-orange. Over and over again. Flashes of yellow, red, orange. Bright, beautiful lights moving rapidly from me into space like when a space ship hits warp speed in the movies. I don't know how long it lasted, but I remember it quite vividly.

The next thing I remember was warmth like I had never felt before. I was being lowered into water that was warm...a very relaxing, soothing warm.

Then I heard voices. I squinted and saw a room full of doctors and nurses and who knows who else. They were all chattering and busying themselves around my bed. I opened my eyes fully to see a doctor's face inches from mine.

He looked in my eyes, smiled, and simply said "Welcome back."

Two talented surgeons, countless nurses, four by-passes, a loving family, hundreds of dear friends, thousands of prayers, and a generous and forgiving God gave me a new lease on life. As I walked out of the hospital five days later, I exclaimed to Denise, "It's good to be back." ❊

The Day the Boys Took Flight

BY PETER SNYDER

In the late 1930's my uncle Wesley (Bud) Elliott Jr. and his uncle Keith Kimball, who were about 11 and 15 at the time, had a short lived experience with the art of flying. Keith was like most farm boys of his day, always tinkering with or building something on their farm, 2-3 miles south of Canton. Keith had started to build a glider plane, and along with the help of Wesley they finished the project one weekend afternoon when Wesley's parents, Wes and Pat Elliott, were visiting for the day as they lived close, just east of Harmony on the Coyle farm. The Kimball farm had no hills from which to launch their creation. The boys came up with the next best thing to a hill—the barn.

Somehow the two hauled the glider to the top of the barn before either set of parents had seen what they were up to, for they surely would have put a stop to such nonsense. As luck would have it, a decent summer afternoon breeze had come up. The boys launched their creation. It was a glorious success. The glider caught the wind and took off to the delightful hollering of Keith and Wesley. The noise got the attention of their parents, who came around the house just in time to see the boys fly over the farmstead heading out towards the pasture.

Now Keith's father was already a man in his sixties and Keith was the baby of the family, so my great-grandfather started to run after the boys shouting "Keithey, my Keithey! Oh my precious Keithey! God save my baby," never acknowledging that his grandson was also a passenger on this contraption. The boys' flight ended about a hundred yards from where it started with a not-so-gentle landing in an old apple tree. By the time Keith's dad arrived at the tree, well-winded, the boys had extracted themselves from the glider and the tree, none the worse for wear. After seeing the boys were unharmed (mainly Keith) Great-Grandpa was quite angry. He doled out punishment for the boys, went and retrieved an axe, and proceeded to chop the glider to bits. ✳

Christmas Eve 2003

By Herb Highum

This happened to me on Christmas Eve. My wife, Ruby, suffered a heart attack on December 18, 2003 and was taken by ambulance to the Winona Memorial Hospital. After a few days of touch and go she started to get better. By Christmas Eve she had progressed, so I did not stay overnight at the hospital.

I had gone to church in Rushford at 4:00 p.m. and to birthday dinner at our son, Kenny, and his wife, Toni's, home, as it was grandson Jacob's birthday. I got back to Winona about 6:30. I stayed with Ruby until after visiting hours. I was feeling sorry for myself as I walked to the parking lot to get into my car. I turned up to look at the window where Ruby was in the ICU and thought what a bum Christmas this was—Ruby up there, and for the first time in 51 years we could not be together.

At that moment there was some noise behind me and I turned to see a young man on a motorized wheelchair go by. He had no legs. I looked up at the heavens and said, "Okay, God, it could be worse."

Just when we are feeling sorry for ourselves, we are shown something to remind us that God is with us. ✳

Missing the Bus

By Tim Gossman

I grew up on a family farm in south central Minnesota near the town of Alma City. When I was in grade school, I loved to get up early in the morning to see what the new day would bring. When I became a teenager and went to high school it was a different story and it was difficult for me to get up in the morning. At this time my sister, Sue and my older brother, Dan had graduated and moved out of the house and I shared a room with my younger brother, Scott. Every morning before my mom, Lois, left to work the early shift at the Cool Whip factory, she would wake up Scott and me to tell us good by, but I did not *have* to get up then. Later, my dad, Joe, would come in from chores and call for me to get up and usually call several more times before I finally drug myself out of bed. Sometimes even his best efforts calling from the bottom of the stairs would not get me going and suddenly I would see him standing at the foot of my bed saying, "If you don't get up now you will miss the bus!"

In 1981 I married my college sweetheart, Susan, and we moved to Fillmore County near Wykoff. Next we lived in Chatfield and then near Washington and finally settled on our farm near Chatfield. My daughters, Sophia and Sarah were born in 1985 and 1988. In 1996 my dad passed away.

In 2000, Sophia and I were going on the 9th grade class trip to Washington D.C. with Dave Zimmer. An early start was planned for the day we left, with the buses scheduled to leave Chatfield High School at 5:30 am. I set the alarm for 4:00, when I planned to get up, do chores, get everyone else up and head to town. I slept soundly, and when the alarm went off, I shut it off and fell back asleep. The next thing I knew, I saw my dad standing at the foot of the bed saying, "If you don't get up now you will miss the bus!" I bolted upright, looked at the clock and it was 5:00! When I turned to look back, he was gone. I woke everyone up, and we headed for Chatfield, where Sophia and I just caught the bus and Susan and Sarah returned home to do the farm chores.

To this day I do not know if my dad came to me in a dream or as a spirit. I do know that he came back to help me out one more time, to keep me from missing the bus! ✳

Hello, Central?

By Cheryl Serfling

In the mid 1950's when my sisters and I were all teenagers, except our youngest sister who was around five, we were left alone on a Saturday night. Now that wasn't unusual because our mother had passed away and Dad always went to the Cherry Grove store to get our weekly $7.50 worth of groceries and visit.

This night we had just turned off all the lights and were headed for bed when a noisy car drove in. Knowing it wasn't Dad, we looked out to see who was coming so late. Now this was before security yard lights, so all we caught was a glimpse of two men with guns. They disappeared into the barn.

Our kitchen had six huge windows in it and we thought if shots were going to be fired we'd better start crawling on the floor. We managed to get the doors locked but how do you talk on the hand crank wall phone without standing up?

My oldest sister finally got brave enough. While we peeped out the windows, she rang central and our Great Uncle Walt, who ran the switchboard in Cherry Grove, quickly answered. She told him of our situation, and he told us to sit tight, he'd be right there.

We waited for what seemed ages, but was actually just long enough for Walt to go to the grocery store and pick up a car load of men, and drive two miles.

The men cautiously got out, flashlights in hand, and walked around the yard. Finally they saw a faint light coming from the hay mow, so Uncle Walt went to the barn, turned all the lights on and bellowed "What ya doing up there? Get down here now!" Now Uncle Walt was a school bus driver and if he told you to do something, you pretty much did it. Now.

Down came the neighbor's boy and their new hired man. They were hunting pigeons. Uncle Walt gave them one of his stern lectures about holes in the barn, not asking permission, and scaring the living daylights out of us girls.

Another hunting trip run afowl. ✳

Adventures in Driving

By Erik Paulson

It's a tradition in the rural areas of the United States for a father to take his son or daughter out for their first driving lesson. Some of us start a little younger than others, and a few of us are lucky to be given a second lesson after the first. Fewer of us are fortunate enough to have a parent who's a driver education instructor. Such was my case on all three counts. Still, my first experience behind the wheel is a memorable event and one to be noted, considering that I almost wrecked the car.

I still don't know why, but in the summer of 1987 or '88, Dad decided to supplement our vehicle fleet with a 1976 Oldsmobile station wagon. It was the epitome of the term "land yacht," painted a dark, metallic blue with a black interior and had that God-awful fake wood paneling on the side (I loathe fake wood paneling on cars more than vinyl roofs). Best of all, it had the famed Oldsmobile 455 "Rocket" V-8 under the hood. However, it wasn't the excess horsepower that almost ended my driving career—it was my ignorance of local geography and landmarks.

My first lesson took place at the community garden below the sewage treatment plant and adjacent to the fair grounds in Preston. Dad had a plot there and many a summer afternoon was spent sitting in the car (I sunburned easily and needed to stay in the shade), with the doors and windows open, listening to music on my headphones or reading a book while Dad tended to his crops. One afternoon, I talked Dad into letting me drive the car from the path that encircled the garden and up the gravel access road to Fillmore Street. He reluctantly agreed.

Since I was only twelve, and a great deal shorter than my father, I sat on the edge of the driver's seat so I could reach the pedals and Dad handed me the keys. I remember the rush I got as I pumped the accelerator, turned the key, and had that 455 growl at my command. I put my foot down to edge forward, but the engine had enough power to propel the car on its own. It had been raining earlier in the day and a large mud puddle obstructed our path, so I had to choose to veer left into the garden, veer right into a path of weeds or give 'er the gun and go through the puddle. Dad told me to turn to avoid the puddle and not to go left into the garden, which left me with only one option...the weeds.

Now, being as young as I was, I was unaware that the long disused city ice skating rink was located in that area and there was an earthen barrier that surrounded it, which had been obscured by the weeds. Shortly after I steered right to avoid the puddle, the world tilted about thirty degrees, as the tires climbed the berm. I sat there dumbfounded as Dad frantically reached across the twelve feet of seat and dashboard to crank the wheel, screaming "Turn! Turn! Turn!" or something to that effect. He finally got the car righted, and I drove the rest of the way to Fillmore Street without incident.

Needless to say, it was a while before Dad and I went driving again. ✳

Pride Goeth Before the Fall

By Jeff Kamm

It was a hot spring morning by Minnesota's mid-May standards. The Trout Trot, as the race is called, is an annual rite of spring in the beautiful town of Preston in southeastern Minnesota. This particular race was special because it would be my first foot race of the summer. Now for some reason, I am not always sure why, ten years back I established for myself a running goal. I would run 200 races by my 60th birthday. I have averaged ten to fourteen races a year. At present count, I had run 157 races with three years to go before my 60th birthday. Until this particular race, I was pretty sure I was going to achieve my goal.

I was anticipating this race to be average at best. The Trout Trot Run was a race that just happened to work into my weekend schedule, and because it was my first race of the season, the race felt a little more festive than most races. In any case the whole race was unfolding pretty routinely. After a modest attempt at warming up, and even a more feeble attempt at stretching winter tightened muscles, I made my way to the starting area. I don't remember anything special about how I felt physically that day.

I know the pre-race routine by heart. I found my pre-race starting position, approximately in the middle of the pack. Again I made some modest attempts at warm up stretches, mostly for show. I remember looking around at my fellow middle-of-the-packers. There were a handful of kids, some college students, a couple of housewives, and a few middle aged men determined to lose those winter holiday pounds. These middle aged, weight-loss determined men, stood out like sore thumbs. There should be a law against middle aged men wearing those thin nylon multi-colored running shorts with beer bellies pouring over their waist bands.

The most obvious of all of the middle-of-the-packers are always the new running converts. These newborn athletes looked like refugees from the pre-running movement days. These runners displayed all the tell-tale signs of running rookies. They sported red, white and blue head bands, Bermuda style running shorts, Converse basketball shoes and sleeveless white work t-shirts— clearly running wear of the inexperienced. There is fashion code in running as there with any sport. My remarks are in no way meant to be any sort of criticism or demeaning of my fellow middle-of-the-pack runners. I did say I line up here also.

After the customary fare of thanks to local race sponsors from the community by the race director, and a brief rendition of the "Star Spangled Banner" by the local chapter of the VFW, and of course the introduction of the Dairy Princess, we were ready to start the race. Symbolically, the starting gun was fired by the local District State Representative shouting "go!" And we were off.

The first mile of the race was figuratively all downhill. I felt like I was running on a cloud. I picked up the pace a little, which would not be the norm for my style of running, so I was pleasurably surprised with myself when I did. It felt good.

I am guessing now, but I am pretty sure that I wasn't into the race more than a mile when I first felt a little pressure in the middle of my chest. I slowed my pace and thought to myself, "hmm, that's an odd feeling." I continued to run. The heaviness in my chest didn't go away, but continued to increase, and then there was some pain. I chose to ignore the uncomfortable feeling. At this point in the run, I was still looking good, my stride was decent and my arm action was smooth. But the tautness in my chest was now very quickly turning to real pain and the pressure situation had increased ten fold. I couldn't ever remember having this sensation in my chest. No matter what I tried doing, I couldn't get at ease with my pain. Was this a heart attack? A sick feeling started to overcome me, that hot, sick, sweaty feeling that suggests "this can't be happening to me."

I was experiencing a boatload of distressing sensations. The pain in my chest was now borderline paralyzing. I looked around as I began to slow my pace and further assess my situation. Little kids, old people, and the new running converts flew past me. I thought "gee, I hope these people don't think this is the fastest I can run." Silly, huh?

About twenty-five more yards down the road, and I came to a complete stop. Strangely, I felt embarrassed. I was more concerned with how I might look to the other runners, rather than considering I might be in the middle of having a heart attack. I bent over and straightened up, unable to relieve the pain in my chest or get comfortable. Beads of sweat poured off my forehead, and my T-shirt was soaked. Panic was now running it's own race into my brain. I remember watching my fellow runners go by me, and feeling contempt for all of them. I walked over to the side of the road, still trying to maintain a degree of running poise, all this in spite of the fact I felt more like vomiting, which would be neither cool nor fashionable.

The pain in my chest was now so great I went down to one knee. In the name of appearance, while on one knee, I started to fiddle with my shoe lace, like my shoe lace needed to be retied, all in an effort not to look out of place.

I had to make a choice. Should I fall down to the ground, clutch my chest, roll around and submit to what comes next and forget this pride stuff? Did I really want to have all those strangers looking at me? No! I decided I would stand the pain, and with a great deal of apprehension and anxiety, I turned and started to walk back towards the starting line. It seemed to make sense at the time. As I walked back toward the starting line, runners continued to file past me headed in the opposite direction. I felt a sense of humiliation. If a fellow runner would make eye contact with me as he or she ran past, I would point down and mumble something like, "I twisted my ankle."

Now here comes the crazy part to this race. Once I had caught my breath and started walking back towards the starting line, the pain in my chest began to go away. By the time I was a 100 yards away, the pain was from top to bottom gone. As I approached, some of the race volunteers, they began to suspiciously eye me over. I put my hand in my pocket as if I had something in there, and commented, "pager went off, need to deliver a couple of babies." A race staffer smiled, gave me the thumbs up and waved me off. I walked toward my car parked in the race day assigned parking area. I was stunned by what had just transpired and feeling a lot more than just a little troubled with my future. In the car I checked and adjusted the rear view mirror where I saw the first runners crossing the start/finish line. I felt disgraced. I drove the eight miles home in deep consideration. What had this chest pain meant? Was it an early warning sign of a future heart attack, or was it a product of eating that slightly out-dated tuna sandwich out of the vending machine?

I didn't know the answer, but I knew one thing: what I had just experienced was painful and very scary, and yes, regardless of what kind of spin I may try to put on it, there was a lesson to be learned here. The lesson I learned that day was a simple one that I would like to share.

Every year we hear of people who unnecessarily die in the bathrooms of restaurants. These people aren't dying because the food is bad, but are dying because their pride has gotten in the way of common sense. An EMT friend of mine told me that it's not uncommon to find heart attack victims dead in the bathrooms of restaurants. It seems that these people feel they are having a heart attack at the dining table and, rather than tell someone to call 911 and be embarrassed by all the public hassle, the person will go into the bathroom so they don't disturb anyone, have their heart attack and die. My foolish pride could have also cost me my life at the Trout Trot because I couldn't ask for help. But I will ask for help next time. ✻

The Day the Lights Went Out at Mystery Cave

By Carol Thouin

Looking back at the jobs I held while in high school, I'd have to say that being a tour guide at Mystery Cave ranks among my favorite. I was sixteen when I first landed my job as tour guide, concession stand clerk, grounds keeper and head guano sweeper at one of Fillmore County's leading tourist attractions. Today, the cave system is owned by the Department of Natural Resources. Back then, it was privately owned and a popular hangout for locals.

I was among about a dozen teens that spent their summer leading throngs of sightseers through the damp, dark passageways of Mystery Cave and neighboring Minnesota Caverns. The owner of the cave was a spelunker with the Minnesota Geological Survey and insisted we learn the proper terminology for all the minerals and rock formations and the scientific ways in which the cave system itself was created. Our guests never got the pleasure of seeing where Paul Bunyan cemented his footprint in the cave's ceiling or where the image of Christ's face divinely became etched on one of the cave walls one day. No. We stuck to the script and it was purely factual.

As guides, we took turns working in the concession and souvenir stand and giving tours. Nobody wanted to be the next person up to give a tour close to quitting time. But that's precisely where I found myself that day in the summer of 1973. I've never forgotten it. I had been called to duty at Minnesota Caverns that day. That cave is about a mile, as the crow flies, from Mystery Cave but has a much longer tour route. Pam was one of my fellow guides and was down in the cave giving what we all thought was going to be the last tour of the afternoon. Then, as luck would have it, a couple and their two children slowly poked their way up to the ticket booth. I was swearing under my breath. How could they be so inconsiderate to come this close to my quitting time? I hadn't learned the concept of customer service yet. Finally this family decided they wanted a tour so I forced a smile, grabbed my flashlight and beckoned the family to join me on an exciting caving adventure.

We were about a third of the way into the tour, me touting all the wonders of cave formations I had memorized earlier in the summer, when the lights suddenly went off. When lights go out in a cave, several hundred feet underground, you experience total darkness. It's a kind of darkness where you can't even see your hand if it's touching your face. I turned on my dimly flickering Mystery Cave-issued flashlight that was already seriously low on batteries. My once captive audience had become a little uneasy with our current situation. I assured my tour group that the light controls just down the pathway must have mistakenly been turned off. I asked that they wait for me and that I'd return promptly. I left them in total darkness for what probably seemed to them like an hour, but was only five or ten minutes. I cautiously made my way down the passageway to the next bank of lights. I was relieved to reach the lights and made the switch. Nothing! Still no lights. I had no choice but to return to my group, who were now becoming a bit more panicky. Still trying not to alarm anyone, I told them that I had tried the wrong set of lights. I headed off in a completely different direction, with my ever dimming flashlight, to an opposite bank of lights. When I reached up to pull the switch and got nothing, I knew what had happened. I couldn't tell these poor people that the stupid tour guide before me, thinking she was the last tour of the day, turned off the main power switch to the entire cave. That was something I decided not to share to avoid further panic. By the time I got back to the couple and their kids, they were becoming very nervous and more annoyed with me by the minute. My flashlight had all but given up when I courageously suggested we make our way slowly back to the entrance. I got no arguments. A few steps into our escape, my flashlight died. After a few hearty slams on my palm (a gesture that usually evoked a few more minutes of battery time) there was nothing. We had no light to maneuver our way back to the surface. I'd have to rely on my memory to negotiate our way over bridges, trenches, ditches and other treacheries. At one point I had an epiphany. Maybe these people smoked and had matches! Voila, it was a brilliant idea but worked only until we burned out their only pack of matches while walking a measly twenty feet.

Thinking back, I must have gone into commando mode. I mustered up all the courage I had at age sixteen to safely maneuver my four cave guests—in total darkness—down narrow pathways and over steep embankments. Luckily, I had memorized every nook and cranny of the cave route throughout the summer while giving countless tours. As we got to the long, steep stairway that led to the surface, light was streaming in. We were safe. I felt energized, like a hero, as I led my weary guests back into the souvenir stand. They appeared no worse for the wear after their unusual Minnesota Caverns adventure. Incensed at their shabby treatment, they only wanted a refund and left the premises without as much as a thank you. I, on the other hand, had a story that I could tell—and I told it to all my fellow guides the next day, and to my family, and to my high school buddies and later to my college friends and my husband and my children and anyone else who would listen to the story about my darkest day at Mystery Cave. ✳

Reminiscence

A young Al Mathison with cow.

"Memories of an Indentured Farm Kid"
PAGE 85

Memory believes before knowing remembers.

~ William Faulkner

Memories of an Indentured Farm Kid

By Al Mathison

Most of my memories of growing up on the windswept plains of Carimona Township in central Fillmore County are of ceaseless labor. At least that's what it seemed like at the time. There was no sunup to sundown to our workdays; that would have been like taking a day off. The day started in deep darkness and ended in even deeper darkness. Such was the life of an indentured dairy farm kid back in the 1960s.

It was similar to what I imagine an Amish upbringing to be, only we had been blessed with electricity. We did not milk cows by hand either. We used heavy stainless steel milking buckets that we strapped onto the cows. You had to watch out because the cow would then aim a well-timed and strategic kick straight at your groin. If you lost your temper and kicked back or poked the critter with a pitchfork, you were only asking for more trouble. For cows, as dumb and belligerent as they were, had better memories than elephants, and they would carry a grudge to the end of their milking career. Right up to the moment that they were loaded onto a trailer and sent on their final journey to hamburger heaven.

The daily drudgery of milking was something I neither had the temperament nor the aptitude for. There was no way that I could tell if the udder was half full or half empty. Supposedly, if you left the machine on too long you could ruin the cow's chances of becoming a champion milker, and if you pulled it off too soon, you were leaving unmilked dollars fermenting up inside.

There was undoubtedly tons of information on the technicalities of milking and the finer points of cows as magazines on the subjects arrived regularly in our mailbox. But who wanted to read an article about milking? Cows were oversized brutes, cud-chewing monsters from a nightmare, and I never met one I liked.

On the other hand, my milking bosses, my dad and my grandpa, seemed to love milking. They thrived in the barn—a dusty foul smelling place—like it was in their DNA. I suspected that the men in our family tree, back in Norway over the last 1,000 years, were much the same way. They weren't the Vikings of lore, who conquered and plundered and hedonized everything they came in contact with. No, they were quieter, salt of the earth types. They were milkers.

Once during a break from the daily chores I paged through a National Geographic and I learned that people worshiped cows in India and let them walk around their streets doing whatever they wanted to do. For some reason the people thought their ancestors, after dying, returned to the earth as cows.

Holy Cow! At least I didn't have to deal with that!

* * *

There seemed to be only two seasons during those indentured days and they were called baling season and non-baling season. Baling season stretched from late May to late September. Non baling season was when it snowed.

All the elements of the Universe had to cooperate in order for a perfect bale of hay to be produced: the humidity, the length of day, the amount of sunshine, the temperature, the wind and other obscure karmic forces. In the end, a perfect bale of hay was about as common as a hole in one on a Par 6 at the golf course, but we had neither the time nor the patience for hitting a silly little ball around a manicured pasture. If it was warm and sunny out and the breeze was just right, we were not recreating; we were baling.

We had to maintain several tractors and numerous pieces of unreliable machinery to get the hay ready to bale. First we mowed the hay and let it lay flat so it could dry for a couple days before raking it into a windrow. More often than not, just when we were ready to go out to the field with the baler a big puffy cumulonimbus cloud the size of the entire township would move overhead and all the hay would immediately get tough, which means the bales, instead of weighing fifty pounds, would weigh closer to one hundred pounds. If it rained while the hay was in a windrow we would have to start all over the next day and re-rake it and get ready again to bale before the inevitable clouds ruined another fine haying day. Eventually we'd have to bale it up in whatever shape it was in just to get it off the field.

Once the bales were stacked up in the hay mow, the wet hay would start rotting and in the process get so hot that it was capable of spontaneously combusting. This never happened to us, but you'd hear of it happening somewhere across the Cow and Hay Belt of America almost every summer—fire in the hay mow which quickly led to fire in the barn. If the cows were still in there, they'd be roasted beyond recognition, too charred to even eat.

* * *

I left the dairy farm the first chance I got and was soon headed west. Twenty years old and I had California on my mind. But living near the center of downtown Los Angeles never felt all that natural. Somehow, as improbable and hard as it was to believe, I had farming in my blood. It would be another ten years or so of big city living, as well as a couple years of jungle living in South America, before I got the wanderlust tamed down enough to venture back to Fillmore County; before I would finally accept my fate and destiny and settle down to become the farmer I was meant to be. (Without the dairy cows though.)

I've got a five year-old son now who holds his nose whenever the sweet Carimona country air turns a little too ripe from the numerous concentrated hog buildings of the area. When I call him my little farm boy, he shouts back with rage, "I'm not a farm boy!"

You just wait, I tell him. ✳

Hot Hay!

By Majorie Taylor Smith

My dad was a great soil conservationist years ago when farmers plowed up and down hills, cleared land of trees to plant crops, and wondered why field "washes" so. He spent many an hour persuading landowners in Rush-Pine Watershed to keep the rain where it fell. All too well, those folks who lived in Rushford knew about the floods in spring or after a heavy rain. It was heart-warming to know Dad lived long enough to see the dikes at Rushford dedicated, thereby aiding the land practices in preventing floods in the town.

However, the story I'd like to share is typical of his love for his farm and the land.

It had been a rainy haying season, very hard to get hay dry enough to store. One day's crop, Dad knew, was a little on the damp side. It could "heat" and ultimately burst into spontaneous combustion. So, after the 10 o'clock news he put his shoes back on and trudged up the well-worn path into the hay mow one more time, where the suspect batch lay. He poked a fork down into the pile and it was ashes down there! He called the fire department and alerted neighbors. Boards were removed from the side of the barn and men pushed that hay out of the second story. The hay burst into flame as soon as it hit the air. Tractors with front-end loaders pushed it away as the firemen kept the barn from igniting. They worked for hours. The women brought food and coffee. Finally, what could have been a disastrous fire was the loss of a few boards, one day's hay. It was also a night of neighborly loyalty and support. ❁

Garden Genes

By Ann Marie Lemke

My mother and grandmother have been gardening all their lives. Any flowers or vegetables that can grow in our southeastern Minnesota climate probably have been tried by one or both of them. If anyone ever required that I sum up either of their lives with a single phrase, it would have to be, "She is a gardener."

In my pre-teen years I never would have believed that I would want to—let alone look *forward* to—planting my vegetable garden and tending my ever increasing flower gardens. Some of my earliest memories are tied to working with Mom and Grandma in the gardens. They are also tied to feelings of dread and loathing. I hated having to work in the gardens. Flower gardens were especially hard because the plants which had yet to bloom were hard to differentiate from the weeds, and the flowers were not in neat rows, like the vegetables. So much for hacking away quickly with the hoe to get it over with so I could go play.

When I was small, our vegetable gardens were not very handy. Mom had two; one was shared at the neighboring farm and the other was shared with my grandparents at their farm. We lived in the country, but our place was on a hillside and there wasn't a sunny area flat enough for Mom to plant vegetables.

Sometimes we would bicycle to the garden at the neighbors' farm. Mom would mount her gold Sears 3-speed and I would be placed on the back with a leg in each of the twin carrying baskets that were mounted on the fender. I held our tools and my sister followed after us on her blue single-speed bike with the pump brakes.

At harvest time when more tools than we could carry were needed, Dad would drive us to the neighbors in his red Econoline pickup. My sister and I would ride, rather dangerously, sitting on the open tailgate wondering if our feet would drag in the gravel if we went over any big bumps in the road.

The vegetable garden at my grandparents' farm was a source of nightmares. It must have been an acre in size, or at least seemed so to my pre-kindergarten eyes. The approach was difficult enough. Through the shady apple orchard, past a gate to cross the cow lane, through another gate and there it stretched out before me, so huge I could barely make out the strawberry beds on the far end. Grandma had boards to put down to cross the cow lane without getting covered with manure, but if there was actually a cow using the lane to get from the barnyard to the luscious green pasture that was on the other side of the garden, I was too terrified to cross.

Since my sister and I were young, and supposedly agile, we were often relegated the jobs that required bending over a lot or squatting close to the ground. To us fell the task of picking strawberries, with reminders to pick the plants clean, but also to be careful not to step or sit on them. We also picked pail upon pail of peas, again with orders to pick those plants clean, but also to make sure the pods were full enough and not to eat too many. After receiving "The Look" for the scattered empty pods left between rows after munching, we figured out the wise thing to do was to pitch them over the fence in to the cow pasture.

The most dreaded job, by far, was picking up the potatoes in the early fall. To me it seemed they planted 100 rows. The adults would dig up the hills and let the dirt on the potatoes dry slightly. Then us "youngsters," who could bend and squat more easily, came along and cleaned off the dirt and loaded them into burlap bags, later to be transported to basements for winter storage.

My own adventures in gardening snuck up on me. Once I had an apartment with a balcony providing easy access to the outdoors, I started some pots with flowering plants. Next thing I knew I had planted a pine tree in a pot. Luckily for the tree, I bought my house and the tree now resides proudly in the yard, near to my vegetable garden.

Yes, after all the dread, loathing and complaining of my early years, I planted a vegetable garden of my own. Of course, I have the luxury of size control for my vegetable patch. I'm in charge. I don't know who was more surprised when I decided to dig out some sod to put in a garden: me, or my parents when I asked them to bring their tiller over.

The flower garden projects seem to grow exponentially every year I live here. Tulip and daffodil bulbs went in the first fall. More sod came out to connect two smaller flower gardens to a larger one to which I added a stone path and birdbath. I tend the plants left behind by previous owners and add more of my own every year along with donations from family members.

I've finally found what my mother and grandmother have known all along, that joy and peace can come from acknowledging the garden genes and tending the good soil. I find satisfaction in the sight of freshly turned, weed free soil. I lose all track of time and all weight of worries when I'm working in the garden. I look forward with great anticipation to those quiet summer evenings with soft breezes when I can abandon the cares of the world and tend new life—in my garden. ✳

A Mother's Fear

BY HERB HIGHUM

Do you remember Pearl Harbor? I sure do! That Sunday, December 7, 1941, began as most days in America. My folks took me (age 13) and my younger brother Glenn (age 10) to Sunday School and church in Rushford. I also had three older brothers, George M. (age 22), Robert (age 25), and Asmund (age 27), but they were not at home that I recall.

We came home from church and, as was the custom, we turned on the radio to get some news. Radios in cars were a rare thing in those days. The news was on, and we heard that Pearl Harbor had been attacked and we would surely go to war! We stopped what we were doing to listen. The news didn't get any better. We were at war!!

I remember thinking that Hawaii was a long ways away, so why was Mom sobbing and crying while she fixed dinner? We had dinner and helped Mom with the dishes, but she continued to be so sad. Nothing we said could cheer her up.

World War II took place on the world stage right before our eyes but finally ended in 1945. My oldest brother Asmund served in the U.S. Army in Morocco. Rob was a valuable farmer so he was never called. George M, had back surgery when only eight years old so he couldn't serve. I graduated in 1946 and was never drafted, and Glenn served in the army after graduating from Luther College in 1953.

But getting back to Mom—it was several years later that I realized why she was so sad that fateful day. She was the mother of five sons and feared the loss of any. ✻

A Railroader's Daughter

BY MARJORIE EVENSON SPELHAUG

I was fortunate to grow up in Whalan, Minnesota, at a time when a great number of trains would be going through town. My dad, A.M. Evenson, was an employee of the C.M. St.P.&P. Railroad for over forty-five years. Many of those years were on the Southern Minnesota Division from Austin to La Crosse, Wisconsin. Up to about age ten, I rode on a train more often than in a car.

There was a diesel train that had a passenger car, mail car, and the diesel engine. My Dad called this small train "The Galloping Goose." This Passenger train stopped in Whalan at 11:00 a.m. on its way to La Crosse. My Mom and I would often take this train to La Crosse to go shopping. What fun! We stopped at all the towns along the way, picking up more passengers.

When we arrived at the Big Brick Depot in La Crosse, we hurried up the steps to the viaduct where there was a street car stop. We boarded the changing street car and went across the causeway to downtown La Crosse to do our shopping.

I especially remember going to either Kresge's or Woolworth's and having a banana split. It was so good, but it cost $.10 which was quite expensive then. After we were through shopping we met the street car at the Fannie Farmer Candy Store Corner to go back to the depot to catch a train to Whalan. ❋

Spring Banquet

By Carol Hahn Schmidt

It was the spring of 1931 and time for the junior/senior banquet. I was a senior that year at Preston High School. The banquet was being served in the high school gym by one of the churches' Ladies Aid. Back when we were juniors we did an unheard of thing and had the banquet at the Kahler Hotel in Rochester. The churches had complained, as it was one of their ways to make money, so in our senior year the banquet was again being held in Preston.

These were prohibition days and pre-dancing days—the days of the Puritan Twins: Penelope and Prudence. Anyone who even thought the word "dancing" was evil. School proms came much later. We had our banquet dresses on and were looking forward to it just as students look forward to prom today. Our class colors were orchid and yellow, so the crepe paper streamers were orchid and yellow, and table decorations were our own lilacs and tulips. It was the Great Depression and money was scarce. The lattice and arch were also decorated with flowers, which had been gathered from people around Preston. It was 1931, a much simpler time, and we thoroughly enjoyed this grand occasion. ❀

Feathered Friends

By Bonnie Heusinkveld

My childhood was spent on a farm near Cherry Grove, on the place where I was born. My family was quite different than the families of my friends. I was an only child. At the time, I didn't know what I was missing. As I grew up and married, I learned many of the things that I never experienced: the camaraderie of brothers and sisters, the antics they pull on each other and the compassion they have for one another, at least most of the time.

However, I was not lonely. I had my pets. Our farm had the usual dog and cats, but I tamed chickens, hens to be exact. Today, we would call them range chickens. They were free to roam the barnyard and even the lawn by the house. My pets, I believe, were Plymouth Rocks. We also had Leghorns, but they were hard to catch.

After holding them and petting them a few times, I could pick my chickens up anywhere in the yard. I gave them all names, too. I remember Myrtle, Mathilda and Purple Tail. I could give Mathilda and Purple Tail rides in my wagon or pull them on a sled. I usually had to lift them off; they didn't jump off or fly away. In the winter months, they were confined in the chicken coop. They really seemed to enjoy the rides. Maybe it was better than being "cooped up."

These feathered friends were also my guests for tea at my playhouse in an empty corncrib. I still marvel at how I could set them on makeshift chairs at a table and they would sit there. The chairs were fashioned from old boards put across wood blocks that my dad had not yet split for use in the stove in the house. The table was a half-barrel placed upside down. Our menu usually consisted of corn or wheat on a plate. I served water in the cups. I thought a little dirt in the water looked more like tea or coffee, but they just wouldn't drink it. I can't remember ever having to clean up after my guests. They must have used the outdoor facilities. They weren't very excitable when I was alone with them.

As I grew older, part of my chores was to help with the chickens. By then, my pets were gone and I had friends in school. I didn't mind gathering eggs, but I detested washing them.

The first years my husband and I were married, chickens were a part of our farm. As a good wife, I did the chicken chores. My love for washing eggs did not grow. My early obsession with feathered friends also diminished. ✳

The Wheelchair Ride

BY CAROL HAHN SCHMIDT

I t had been my wish to see the Harmony-Preston Valley Trail ever since it had been completed, but physically I knew I would never make it on my own. This was the old railroad bed behind my childhood home, where we'd played and walked to school. When my son Dave and his wife Jeanette offered to take me on a wheelchair ride on the trail, I jumped at the chance.

It was the last Sunday in May of 1999 and a windy but gorgeous day. They loaded the wheelchair in the car and Gerald took us out to the Maust Bridge, where we started on the blacktopped trail along Camp Creek going toward Preston. We wheeled through the Maust pasture by the old Berland place, everything gone now except the remodeled house. Here my mind drifted back to childhood days and playing with the Berlands. There were five of them: Lawrence, Paul, Joseph, Marie and Alfred, and the youngest six of us Hahns: Clara, Carol, Nellie, June, Alice Mae, and James. I can see our group sitting under the trees in their yard. One day a long haired, scruffy looking man walked up from the creek bank, came into the yard, and planted himself right in our midst. He began to question us about school. He wanted to know what literature we were studying in English. We answered "Romeo and Juliet." He then quizzed us about the characters and plot. We finally got up and left. We later learned that his name was Hauck. In the summer he lived in a shack along Camp Creek on Goldsmith's land. He had a doctorate degree and taught English and literature at the University of Minnesota. He loved nature but also loved to eat at Mrs. Goldsmith's and Mrs. Berland's tables.

As we wheeled near the creek, I tried to decide where it was that the wagon path narrowed between the bluff and creek—where the boys put the dead snake just to hear the girls scream. We crossed the trail bridge where the railroad bridge was once washed out in the biggest flood we had ever seen in Camp Creek valley. To the right was the line fence and gate between the farms—a favorite spot for our wiener roasts and picnics. Memory fails me—where did we ever get money to buy wieners, buns, and marshmallows? Here we fished and waded in the creek. None of us ever learned to swim. It was here that we played games like "Last Couple Out", "Kick the Can", "Cricket", "Ante-I-Over," "Run Sheep Run." Ball games were also played and we challenged each other to see who could walk the rail the farthest without stepping off.

A wonderful part of a wheelchair ride is that it stops on command. I looked to the right and we were at the meadow. I couldn't believe that I was seeing it again—the meadow where my grandparents had lived. The house foundation was still there and every year poppies, larkspur and daisies would still bloom, planted long ago by my Grandmother Magdelene Hahn. The huge elm trees are gone, as are the giant willows. We played in this meadow and picked early spring flowers and wild strawberries. We knew where the best grapes grew along with plums, gooseberries, and elderberries.

Pushing on we caught peeks of the big white house on top of the hill, which was my childhood home. Familiar places raced through my mind—the porch, the privy, the sand pile, the apple orchard, the swings and hammock, the pump, the well house and on and on.

Cedar trees had grown up and covered the outcropping of rocks by the driveway. I could still feel the excitement we felt when we heard the train whistle at Weigand's crossing. We'd race out to the big rock to wave at Uncle Levi Kline, who was the conductor on the train. He'd wave and blow the whistle at us. We all loved Uncle Levi.

The railroad bridge by the meadow, where we used to step up on the pilings to get onto the tracks, is gone and now replaced by a big culvert. The blacktopped trail didn't even have a bump where we once mounted the bridge.

The long, steep driveway to my old house was in the same place. I could see my sister Luella having to wait for my little legs to catch up, going up that hill. I preferred walking with Clifford as he had time to pick up a stone or a frog or wooly bear caterpillar.

Now came the greatest surprise. The huge bluffs we called the "crocus bluffs," straight up from the railroad tracks, were now covered with scrub trees and shrubs. In our day they were barren. The section men used to burn them off every year to keep the trees and brush from growing.

Pushing on we came to Weigand's pasture. There again the huge old elm trees were gone. It was here in this pasture under those giant elms the Evangelical Church used to hold its annual church picnic. In this part of the creek the kids used to catch crabs, skip rocks and wade up to their waists.

When we came to Camp Creek Bridge we decided to continue onto the Trailhead in Preston. We viewed the fairgrounds from a different angle. The Wolf house is gone, making room for the waste treatment plant, and the pasture is now part of the fairgrounds.

We crossed the bridge to the parking lot, where our ride was waiting for us. Somehow I wasn't there yet. I just wanted to sit alone awhile and digest this extra special trip back into my childhood, a part of me that no one but my sisters would understand. ❋

A Tractor Story

By Richard Prinsen

I'm sure that all of you farmers who grew up in the beginning of "the tractor era" are amazed at what the tractors of today can do. It's almost limitless. They are big, noisy and some are green and they are something to admire, that is until you meet one of them on a country road. Then you wish you had taken another road.

One of the things that hasn't changed is the desire to plow a straight furrow. Farmers all take pride in seeing how straight they can make those furrows. Maybe this had started with who had the best team of horses way back when.

Plowing with a tractor when I grew up wasn't all that great. I could sing to myself or whistle or just sit there and get stiff. One day when I was out plowing a neighbor started plowing next to the field I was plowing. I waved to him as a sign that we were all alright at our house and hoped he and his family were, too. He waved back. He was my friend, Bob Wilson, working for his dad, too. That was a little change in the boredom, but then I got an idea.

The next time I saw Bob, I stood up on the tractor platform and started to wave my arm and then both arms. I waved like mad and then I started pointing in every direction as if something was out there. He was looking in all directions, but couldn't see anything. Every direction he looked, the tractor went that direction, too. There went his straight furrows. Quitting time came and I went home, forgetting about the break in the boredom.

The next morning Dad went to the field and stayed out until

noon, but when he came in he said, "I don't know what was the matter with Bob Wilson. When he saw me coming, he stood up and started waving his arms and pointing in all directions. I couldn't see anything that he was pointing at. I don't know what he was up to."

Then I had a confession to make. ✳

Food

A rooster patrols the henhouse.

"Broken Eggs"
PAGE 108

*"If more of us valued food and cheer and song
above hoarded gold,
it would be a merrier world."*

~ J.R.R. Tolkien, *The Hobbit*

Buying and Selling with Susie

By Anna Rae Nelson

I loved growing up in rural Fillmore County. I grew up on a ridge near Peterson. My mother, Sylvia Passow, has always had horses. As kids, my sister and brother and I had it all—lots of acres to run on and plenty of horses and ponies to run with. I think most of my fondest memories include our Pony of America "Susie" hitched to the little wagon-cart.

In the summer, when the wild plums would ripen, my siblings and I would drive Susie up and down our township road to find the plums growing next to the roadway. We would take plenty of bread bags and fill them full of the juicy plums. Then, it was time for our version of a lemonade stand. We would drive Susie and the cart the mile-and-a half down to Highway 16 and sell the bags of plums to anyone who would stop to see what we were up to.

One of Susie's other chores was to carry us the three miles down the road to our neighbor's dairy farm. We usually bought our milk from them straight from the bulk tank. Of course back then it was common and there were no laws that prevented farmers from selling to anyone other than their contracted buyer. We would fill large jugs with the thick creamy milk and then drive Susie ever-so-carefully back home so as not to spill the milk in the back of the cart.

Susie didn't even get a break in winter time. The best thing to do on a snowy morning with no school? Hook Susie to the long wooden toboggan. I usually got to ride Susie and Sarah and DeLane would ride on the toboggan. Of course it was my job to steer Susie over the highest snow drifts as fast as possible and see how long it would take to unseat my beloved brother and sister. I smile just thinking of the laughter and fun. ✳

Great-Uncle Richard and the Oatmeal Cookies

By Rose Breitsprecher

It was fair time in the early 1960's for a Norway Go-Getters 4-Her. The brown swiss calf was clipped and ready to be shown. The pig was looking long and lean. The butterflies and bugs looked beautiful in a glass-covered case. The dress was pressed and ready to be scrutinized by an eagle-eyed judge.

Entry day dawned and it was time to bake oatmeal cookies. After the batch of cookies were baked, four perfectly uniform cookies were finally selected and placed on a plate. It was then that I made my first mistake. I decided to show my perfect cookies to my Great-Uncle Richard, who was visiting us from California. My second mistake was waking him from his morning nap. He sat up and looked at the cookies. In a blink of an eye, he took a cookie and proceeded to take a big bite out of it. He said they really tasted good. I couldn't believe what he had done. I ran back to the kitchen and showed my mom and sisters the threesome, that was once a perfect foursome. The search was on for a second set of cookies.

I don't remember what kind of ribbon I received on my cookies that year, but I sure remember the day Great-Uncle Richard ate my fair entry. ❁

Broken Eggs

By Peter Snyder

It was 1931, the country was in the throngs of the Great Depression. My father, Robert J. Snyder, lived at the edge of Preston with his parents, Clair Snyder and Nellie Gossman Snyder, and his seven siblings. Like many women of the era, my grandmother supplemented the family income by collecting and selling eggs from her flock of chickens.

My father's job each morning after breakfast was to collect the eggs. It was a good job for an eight year old boy whose older sisters didn't care for the occasional peck of a hen that wasn't so willing to give up her eggs. One morning in a rush, as young boys tend to do, he forgot the egg basket, a metal wire basket that you now see in antique stores sold as a decoration. By the time my father realized he didn't have the basket, he was already at the hen house and didn't want to walk back down the hill about seventy-five yards to the house.

My father decided he was in great luck. He had on a pair of overalls. He promptly filled every pocket available with eggs and proceeded to trot back down the hill to the house. Then it happened. My dad fell down and since he was on a slope he rolled. Needless to say every egg was broken and dad was a sticky, gooey mess of broken eggs. Dad slowly picked himself up and went to the kitchen where he got a good scolding from his mother for the loss of income and the potential ruining of his clothes, followed by a "whipping" by his dad for his carelessness.

Shortly after this incident, my grandfather decided dad would be of more use to him at the apple orchard, Snyder's Orchards, now Pine Tree Apple Orchard. ✳

A Disappointing Watermelon

By Ida Mae Bacon

My dad owned a big pickup truck, and I would ride in the back when I went with my parents.

One day we went to visit my Uncle Louie on his farm. When we were getting ready to leave, he gave us a big watermelon to take home. It was put in the back with me watching it so it wouldn't roll around and break open.

On the way home we stopped to see my dad's cousin. The Stubbes were like hillbillies and let their chickens and animals have free reign. When we went into their house, there were chickens walking on the table. I have a weak stomach and really had a hard time ignoring all that. Then! My dad offered to share our 'precious' watermelon with them. He got it out of the truck, brought it into the house and plunked it right onto the chicken-laden table. I almost lost everything right there. Mrs. Stubbe got her knife, wiped it off on her apron and proceeded to slice the melon. I could have cried! Needless to say, I did not eat any of that watermelon.

On the way home in the back of the truck, I did cry. ✳

Do-It-Yourself Groceries

By Kathleen Mulhern

Butchering on the farm, when we were growing up, was a fact of life if you wanted a variety of meat and to eat well. And eat well, we did!

But it took hard work, grit and sometimes tears. As a preteen and teen, and being the oldest of my siblings, I had to help with the actual butchering of the hogs to get the blood for blood sausage, which was a favorite variety of processed meat. My folks made it my job to catch the blood, and being very sensitive to any type of cruelty, this was almost more than I could handle. Each time I would cry and beg to be let off. But it would never happen. After all, if I wanted to be a nurse, I'd better get used to the sight of blood, they said. I believe all of this was hard on Dad, too, as he always treated animals well. But being the no-nonsense, very disciplined German, he faced reality and did what was needed.

So Mother would hand me a flat bottomed enamel pan in which she had put a handful of course salt and a wooden spoon. After Dad had shot and stabbed the pig, I had to hold this pan to catch the blood, set it immediately on the snow to cool while stirring quickly so it wouldn't curdle.

Mom always insisted that the butchering be done at the full moon so the animal would bleed well and she would have enough to make good blood sausage. We thought it was an old wives' tale, but I read a few years ago that some believe there is validity to it, and some surgeons will not operate during a full moon.

The blood was then cooled to make the blood sausage and can it. This meat only needed to be heated in a frying pan. It was occasionally used for the family supper, or occasionally when unexpected company came. Over the years, many different people ate it, and everyone liked it.

Butchering time, which happened three times a winter, was hard work and hated by us children. I dreaded coming home from school when the kitchen was greasy and messy. I remember helping wherever I could, and my right hand would get sore from hours of hand grinding the fat to render into beautiful, white lard.

But the eating was wonderful! Besides the fresh meat, Mom and Dad also made liver sausage and fried-down meat, and the best meat of all: cured and smoked sausage links, bacon and hams. Hams were made by first soaking them in a salt brine and then hanging them from the rafters of the smoke house. They kept a stove in the center of the room that burned wood chips and corn cobs. Mom also made head cheese and pickled pigs' feet.

To add to our meat supply, we also raised 25-30 roosters to butcher the two days after Thanksgiving. Making us spend vacation days doing this job that we hated was Mother's way to make us love school!

Although some of our neighbors butchered a beef, we never did. Mother bought all the beef we needed from the butcher shop.

None of this have I ever done myself, and I marvel at all the work Mom and Dad did. For us, all this ended with the advent of the meat locker.

Like most women of the time, Mom also preserved the usual fruits and vegetables with one notable addition: for many years we had both a large strawberry and raspberry patch and picked them almost daily.

As Mom had to feed at least two hired men plus her own family of seven, she felt she needed lots of sauce, jam and jelly to go with her homemade bread. So besides eating these fresh berries three times a day in some form, she made so much jam and jelly that she used gallon jars rather than those cute little jam jars. That took a lot of berries. Each year Mom preserved at least thirty-five quarts of raspberry sauce—the best of all the fruit sauces.

In retrospect, I realize that a good share of our waking time for the entire year was needed and used for some type of food preservation, both for humans and for animals, and we children were all involved. We never dreamed of using the phrase, "I'm bored," as we knew the situation would be quickly remedied with a job to do. ✻

Characters

Glenn Brink, "Grandpa"

"There He Is"

PAGE 125

"Some cause happiness wherever they go;
others whenever they go"

~ Oscar Wilde

Starter Fluid

By Wallace Osland

E ach town has people that give it its local color. The opinionated, the busybody, the grapevine gurus who don't hesitate to let you know what they think or to be the first to arrive on the scene to pump you for information so they can broadcast it to everyone else. There are the folks who know how to get things done, and do so, even if it means using both orthodox and unorthodox methods.

Upon my arrival to the Jorris Funeral Home in Spring Valley as a freshly minted mortician out of the University of Minnesota, I soon realized that all of those characteristics, and more, were embodied in Elizabeth Sibigtroth. Elizabeth was in charge of picking up burial permits and paying the gravediggers for burials at Etna Cemetery in rural Spring Valley.

Whenever a death occurred, and the deceased was to be buried at Etna, a safe bet would be to assume that Elizabeth's cream colored '59 Chevy would be parked in back of the funeral home by the time we returned from making the call. Before I even knew any service information, Elizabeth would want to know the date and time of service and burial and when would I be getting the grave dug.

In a very short period of time I learned the ritual of funerals with burials at Etna Cemetery. Elizabeth would be waiting at the funeral home for us, asking her questions about arrangements, and picking up the burial permit and the check for the gravedigger the day following the burial.

But, I remember one interesting exception to this routine.

Shortly after I assumed ownership of the funeral home, I received notification of a death and the deceased was to be buried at Etna Cemetery. Sure enough, Elizabeth was waiting in her '59 Chevy when I returned and stayed there until I was able to answer her questions about the funeral arrangements.

And, like clockwork, she came by the day after burial to pick up the burial permit and Woody's grave digging check. I gave her the check and the permit, but then she gave me an additional bill—for a fifth of whiskey. I paid her out of petty cash, smiled and wrote "starter fluid for grave digger" in the ledger. ❋

Almost Mud Time

By Mary Lewis

When Clint speaks it is with a glint in his eye and tobacco juice on his chin.

"Would you like a little lunch?" he says.

It is 4:00 in the afternoon, but I've learned that a little lunch is different from lunch, and that what you eat at noon is dinner. Knocking snow off my boots, I duck through the door into the dark kitchen and unload my armful of firewood next to the cookstove. I peel off my sweatshirts that smell of chainsaw fumes. We've been cutting up old barn boards back by the corn crib.

Mabel has a big pot of oatmeal cooking for the barn cats on the stove. She gets out bologna and Wonderbread and takes the pot of boiled coffee off the front burner. It's the kind you strain through your teeth.

"Come sit," says Mabe, as she shuffles to the table with the coffee. It's hard for her to straighten up anymore, but I have never heard her complain about her health.

My lower back eases into the angle of the chair and the smell of coffee fills my head. Sawing is tough on the back. I take a sip of the coffee, thick as silt. Mabe puts egg shells in the pot to cut the bitter.

"Are you warmed up Mary?" she says, "Wind's kinda nasty out there. I always know cuz those branches hit the window of the bedroom upstairs. That scrapin's enough to make me feel cold all by itself."

119

"I'm good and warm now Mabe, thanks to that fine fire and your coffee. Old barn wood's pretty dry. Nice spread you laid out here."

"Wish I could give you some preserves from down cellar, I got lots of strawb'ry and plum too, but haven't been down those stairs for a long time."

I helped Mabe with her strawberry bed last summer, intense morsels of flavor here and there among the lanky vigor of quack and lambsquarters.

"Good to be out o' the wind," says Clint. "Can't seem to keep warm like I used to."

He had worn a seed cap with flaps and a strap under the chin, a thinnish jacket that was probably blue once, and fuzzy yellow chore gloves. His nose had dripped from the end as he held boards for me to cut.

"You ought to put on another layer or two Clint, keep you nice and toasty", I say.

"Can't have all that stuff in my way when I'm doin' chores," says he.

"How's the road Mary, drifting up pretty bad?" says Mabel.

"Not so much now, thawed yesterday and that settled it down. But now it's icy. Yesterday when I went out to the mailbox I stood on the ice in the middle of the road just to see what would happen. Wind blew me right across to the other side without me taking a step. Got to remember that when I'm driving on it, especially with no load. I'm kinda looking forward to mudtime."

"That could be any day now, it's prettanear the middle of March already." says Mabe.

"Hauling in mudtime was the worst," says Clint. He slowly shook his head as he peered into his coffee cup that he cradled in both hands. "Many's the time the wheels sunk to the hubs. I'd have to pull off all those cans and whup my poor horse till the wagon pulled free. I been all around this county haulin' milk. Lillie's store down in Amherst used to be a creamery, did you know that Mary? Now Mabe makes me haul milk for those fool cats, nice warm milk and oatmeal. Those critters eat better'n we do."

Mabe and I exchange glances as she opens a pickle jar. She's heard his stories, too.

"One spring when we lived down the hill the crick went from one side of the valley to t'other." says Mabe. "Pasture all under water. Nearly got to the coop, sound of water made the chickens crazy, wouldn't lay for days." She smiles.

"The coop is in great shape, wish I could carry it back to my place and use it for shed space," I say.

Mabe is still smiling, but it is more distant now. Clint shakes his head and rubs his chin.

Happening to glance out the window I see something that propels me out the door like a cannon ball. In an instant I am scrambling to open the door of the moving GMC. If I can't get in, it will roll backward down the hill and crash into the woods in the ravine a quarter of a mile away. I've opened the door but the truck is gaining speed. In a wild jump, I am in the cab. My feet are still dangling out the door, nowhere near the brake. I shouldn't have tried this, now the truck won't be the only thing that's a wreck. I pull my knees in and my left foot hits the edge of the running board. Pushing with all possible force I am upright but still not turned around. The walnut seedlings in the pasture are moving past the window now so we are coming to the steepest part of the hill. Get that right foot out from under the left and apply to the brake. Maybe Clint was right about extra layers; snowpants slowed this operation. Foot on brake at last. Using all restraint, I remember to pump instead of slam. I pump again and again as the truck threatens to enter a sickening slide, tail end trying to be where the front end is. Half way there we come to a stop. We are still on the road, my truck and I.

"Guess I forgot to put her into gear," I say as I reenter the kitchen. "Hand brake's no good."

"Never saw a person move so fast." says Clint. He gives me a good long look. "Had a mare though, got scared of a newspaper blowin' around in the road. Wagon almost off the ground with me in it. Finally slowed down but it took a busted axle to do it. She couldn't drag us home."

121

We eat sugar cookies from the Amherst store, where the creamery used to be.

"Thanks for the lunch." I say.

"Thanks for helping us with that old barn wood," says Clint. "That'll get us through the rest of the winter," says Mabe.

Outside I look out toward the pasturelands flowing into the woods. We are on the crest of a hill in a big bend of the creek that made these lands steep. Simley Creek is hidden beyond the woods and the steep arc of the hill, but I can point to where it curves and I can give you a crow's eye direction for the old homestead. This farm where they now live is a choice site, but I have a feeling that Clint and Mabe will be the last people to live here. The house and barn and corn crib will melt into the earth as their homestead down the hill are doing now. Maybe that is alright. The land will always be here.

I decide to put on the chains, freezing my fingers as I always do. Slowly I pitch down the icy hill, in the right direction this time. ❀

Note: Badgersett borders the land that Clint and Mabel Vickerman lived on, which is now part of the Hvoslef Wildlife Area, once owned by Moppy Anderson of Preston. Moppy's land became that of his son Kinsey and Kinsey's wife Lilia. In 1997 they gave this land they love so much to the state to become Hvoslef Wildlife Area, named after avid Lanesboro naturalist Dr. John C. Hvoslef, 1881-1919. It is a wild and beautiful corner of Fillmore County, now protected from farming and most hunting. Visitors are welcome. Go north on county 23 from 52, just east of Canton. In about 8 miles you come to Amherst. Turn left on the gravel road there which rises up a steep hill. Half a mile on the right is a sign and a parking lot.

Uncle Ingvald

By Signe Housker

Decades ago, one could view a sculpture garden on a farm as one drove from Choice through the South Fork Valley toward Yucatan. The sculptures were created by my uncle, Ingvald Sporgen (b.1876) who immigrated with his parents from Skogdalen on the fjord of Isfjord, across from Andalnes, Norway. They settled on a farm east of the South Fork Church and schoolhouse. A log house was built which still stands. Ingvald's mother died while he was a young boy.

Ingvald was an avid hunter and outdoorsman. He hunted rattlesnakes, collected Indian arrowheads and relics, searched the dry-runs for colorful rocks, and picked blackcaps (berries). It was with the colorful rocks, along with broken pieces of glass, porcelain, and beads, that he created and decorated life-size cement figures of African-Americans, American Indians, Popeye and Olive Oyl, some animals, planters, bird baths, a *kubbe stol* (chair), and a church set in layered rock with flowers.

He started his hobby in the mid-1930's. Ingvald marked his mother's grave with one of his distinctive sculptures.

He had no formal art training or any connection with the art world. It has been said that his creations reminded people of the "grottoes" that became popular in Europe in the 18th century. Ingvald also played the violin without any training.

After his death in 1951, Uncle Ingvald's life works were scattered around the area to relatives and several interested buyers.

In 1997, the Cornucopia Art Center in Lanesboro displayed his art. The exhibit was entitled "Stone by Stone." It was estimated that some of the life-size figures weighed a ton, so moving them involved boom trucks and conveyor belts.

I have many fond memories of my Uncle Ingvald. He was a quiet yet loving and compassionate person who took care of his stepmother (my Grandma) until her death at the age of 94. ✹

There He Is

By John Brink

The day after Grandpa passed away, I was loading manure most of the day. I was thinking of all the things he and I had done together on the farm. I felt a tap on my left shoulder. I turned, but no one was there. I knew instantly that it was Grandpa saying goodbye. I smiled back.

I remember a time long ago when my sister Cherie, dad and I were with Grandpa in the back yard. Grandpa's dog Jacky was there. Cherie was horsing around (as always). Grandpa told Jacky, "Sic her!" and pointed at Cherie. Jacky took after her, but Grandpa knew his dog would not hurt her. Cherie got pretty scared, and then mad. She said, "I can see why you call her a 'pin head dog' when she has a pin head owner!" Grandpa laughed like only he can. And that is one of the things that I miss most about him—his laugh.

When I was young my grandparents, aunts and uncles, and cousins would get together every month at one of our aunt and uncle's houses, or at Grandpa and Grandma's. It was always fun to go to our grandparents' because it was fun to adventure around their farm. In the fall, after (noon) dinner the men and the kids, if we could, would hunt pheasants or squirrels and sometimes fox. In the spring and summer we would often go fishing. These are the times I most enjoyed; my grandpa and my dad both showed me how to tie a knot to tie a fish hook that would always hold. They guided me to the best spots, helped me when my line got tangled up, and taught me how to set the hook on a fish when one did bite.

On one occasion we were at Camp Creek. The fishing was really slow that day. Nothing was biting and I had to go to the bathroom really bad, so my dad took me up in the trees. When we came back, Grandpa said "you better check your pole." I picked it up and I had a fish on, so I set the hook and my Grandpa let out his huge laugh. I pulled in a sucker. I now know that he put him on the hook while I was gone. He just enjoyed seeing his grand kids excited and having fun.

Today was a beautiful Memorial Day so I headed to my favorite fishing hole at the Upper Iowa river. I was sitting on the bank by myself with the river drifting by. I could feel him next to me. And in his whisper, that you can hear a half mile away, he said "there he is." So I set the hook and could hear his laugh. The fight was on. I had hooked into one of the best small mouth bass I have ever caught. I brought it on the bank and was admiring it when I decided that he belonged in the water. I released him.

Then it hit me. Whenever I am alone fishing, and the water is flowing by, and all I can hear is the gentle breeze, or the birds and frogs and fish jumping after insects, I can always feel Grandpa near me.

Now I am soon to be a grandpa myself. I wonder, how can I have such an impact on my grandchild's life as my grandpa had on me? All I know for sure is that I have Grandpa deep in my heart, and that with his example, everything will be fine.

I was just so struck by emotion when I landed the fish that I cried, and I could feel him near me, and I had to write this down. ✳

Reuben's House

By Nancy Overcott

The iron gate wasn't there when my husband and I bought the adjoining property. The present owners installed it long ago, although it seems like only yesterday that I walked up the gateless driveway past the metal mailbox stand that Leland built, past the shed, past the spring where Reuben and Leland fetched their water, and into the yard where sheep grazed and a log house (long since removed) stood attached to the wood frame house where Reuben sat outside in a rickety chair watching a huge, active wasp nest that hung over the door.

Every time I walk past the farm, I think about the way it once was and the way it has changed over the years. When I began my morning walk on January 25, 2003, little did I know that the most dramatic change had just occurred, a change as permanent as death.

I met Reuben Blagsvedt in the spring of 1972 on the day that we began to build a cabin on our land. As refugees from city life, we intended eventually to build a house, grow vegetables, and live as simply and self-sufficiently as possible. Our sixty-two acres in the deciduous bluffland forest south of Lanesboro, known as the Big Woods, suited our purposes, both practically and aesthetically.

When he heard us building our cabin, Reuben decided to visit us. We looked up from our work to see an old man emerging from the woods, walking stick in hand. Speaking softly with a Norwegian accent, although he had been born in this country, Reuben asked, "Who are you then?" After satisfying his curiosity about our intentions, he talked about life in the Big Woods. He told us that he and others owned their own small farms in the area, but that it mostly consisted of small parcels, which absentee owners once used to supply wood for building, heating, and cooking. From the 1920s into the 1960s, many squatters, and some outlaws, lived on these woodlots in small mobile homes or tarpaper shacks and supported themselves by hunting, fishing, growing vegetables, working for local lumbermen, and producing their own supplies of moonshine. By the time we bought our land, no squatters remained, but the woods still had its hillbilly reputation.

After our first meeting, I called on the old man whenever we visited our land, usually bringing him some of my homemade cookies or bread. I also became friends with his son Leland (known as Pancake), a tall thin person with a scraggly beard, who I first saw standing in his doorway holding a shotgun over his shoulder and spitting out a wad of tobacco before saying, "You paid too much for that rough land." Someone once told me that the name Pancake came from Leland's habit of wearing a flat-topped straw hat.

I can still see myself sitting at the father and son's kitchen table drinking coffee boiled over a wood-burning stove, while talking about religion, Garner Ted Armstrong, and social conditions. The house was always cluttered and dirty but the lack of cleanliness only seemed like the outside moving in. The living room, adjacent to the kitchen and the only other room downstairs, contained the one clean thing in the house, a large glass-faced cabinet in which Pancake displayed the Native American arrowheads, utensils, and an intact peace pipe that he had collected over the years. I never ventured upstairs but I think there were two rooms there also.

The disorderliness in which the two men lived may have been due to the absence of a woman. I soon learned that Reuben's wife Lydia had wandered off onto our land just before we bought it, and had frozen to death under a big maple tree. Lydia, the story goes, always thought someone was out to get her.

As time went by, Pancake began to sink into the fogginess of alcohol abuse. While driving drunk on the night of October 5, 1976, he hit another car, killing himself, the driver of the other car, and her three-year-old son. Not long afterward, Reuben died of cancer. The last time I saw him, he was sitting in his log house peeling potatoes next to an oil-burning stove surrounded by old newspapers, magazines, calendars, broken ladders, farming tools, and a clutter of kitchen utensils.

In 1978, after building a house, we moved to our land permanently and I began to take daily walks through the woods and along the township road. The day of my morning walk in January 2003, I had almost reached the bridge that crosses Simley Creek just beyond the old farm when I smelled smoke and looked up to see that Reuben's house was gone! I turned back as though in a dream and walked up the driveway past the mailbox stand, the gate, the shed, and the spring to see what was left. I found only the foundation and the charred remains of two cook stoves, metal chairs, and springs from pieces of furniture. No one was hurt in the fire, as the owners were not living there at the time. I later learned that the sheriff found accelerant in the ashes and determined the fire was the result of arson. As far as I know, the arsonists were never apprehended.

To this day, whenever I pass the farm, I look up and see not just a foundation, but a rickety wood frame house and three people sitting at a kitchen table drinking coffee boiled over a wood-burning stove. ✳

Frank Walsh's Kitchen

By Charles Capek

My cousin Don and I were twelve and thirteen years old the summer we first worked for Frank Walsh. We were restless, full of energy, wanting to explore new worlds and experiences beyond the farm. My uncle volunteered us to help Frank, a reclusive local farmer, get his hay in.

"Frank's just the character to teach you young dogs some new tricks," my uncle said on the drive over. "And you've never been to his place yet!" he said brightly.

We rolled our eyes but kept silent. The July heat was already tiring. And we'd been hired hands often before, with pretty consistent results—hard, dusty work, minimal pay, and worse food. For some reason, folks felt just fine about unloading their stalest potato chips and wateriest Kool-Aid on us.

Frank turned out to be a medium-tall fellow, old, but upright and straight as a rifle barrel, with long, corded arms and hands like a blacksmith—in size, color (dirty), and knobby knuckles. Bright white crew-cut hair, equally bright blue eyes, he had a permanently surprised look to his face. He studied us just as curiously.

"Frank, these are your strong backs and weak minds for the day," my uncle joked by way of introduction. We shook hands, said our hellos, and flexed our muscles, clowning for a bit. Frank had a booming, yodeling voice. "Byyy-yy-y God," he said, raising his eyebrows in amusement at us, "full of kick as colts, are they? We'll see what they're made of."

We walked down to a shimmering, 50-acre hay field that baked in the sun. Oversized, wire-bound rectangular bales sat on the ground where they had fallen from the baler the day before. Frank drove an ancient Case tractor and wagon between rows while Don and I jogged through the stubble and loaded and stacked the bales. When the little tractor began laboring and backfiring from pulling the weight, we headed for the barn.

At the barn, a system of ropes and pulleys and giant iron claws grabbed six bales at a time, which we lifted into the haymow and dropped with a trip switch. There were remnants of a similar system in my uncle's barn, but aside from the Amish farms, Frank probably had the only hand-drawn or horse-drawn haylift in the county.

Not that Don and I had much time to admire it. As soon as the wagon was empty, we went back to the field. After six hours of this back-and-forth routine, our legs were rubbery, our backs and shoulders sore, our hands swollen and rope-blistered (even with gloves), and our forearms hay-pricked and scratched. Our boots felt like hot lead, lined with sandpaper. And we were so dry and thirsty we could barely talk through thickened tongues and cotton mouths.

Frank had heavy streaks of white down his face, where sweat had dried and crusted. He, too, was red-faced from heat and exertion. And even his booming voice was muted.

"Byyy-hy-hy God," he rasped, "let's call that a day and get us some lunch."

Up through the back porch and mudroom he led us, with a full minute's pause while he unlocked, unsnapped, flipped and twisted the 8 different locks he had on the house door. Don and I exchanged looks. Frank was a local legend for his lock obsession. Fuel deliverymen and others entertained café patrons throughout the county with tales of Frank's locks. Now we were among the few to have seen them, and fewer still to pass through them.

Inside, the kitchen was blessedly cool, and Frank invited us to sit at the table while he fetched the lunch. Sitting in the sturdiest of the wobbly, mismatched chairs, Don and I surveyed a kitchen and table like none we had ever imagined. They attested to a lifetime's occupation by a bachelor farmer, with nary the briefest influence of a woman's touch.

On the table, jars of ketchup and peanut butter rubbed elbows with boxes of Ritz crackers and breakfast cereal, a can of coal oil, a small carbon-blackened motor, an empty box and tin foil and dried bones of Banquet Fried Chicken, a package of hot dog buns, and a 50s-era plastic radio. In between these giants, small nuts and bolts and screws and electrical wire and tools lay strewn on stained, oily newspaper, as did several batteries, a corn husking glove, the disassembled parts of a hand planer, and a whetstone. The lone plate had dried layers of countless previous meals on it, and the plate had sat so long in one spot that it had melded to the table finish itself.

The rest of the kitchen was like a living museum, a treasure trove of farm implements and nostrums and advertisements that probably spanned a hundred years. A hand-cranked corn sheller dominated one corner, flanked by several scythes, a post-hole digger, wooden posts, spools of wire, chicken fountains, kerosene lanterns, piles of burlap sacks, horse collars and harness and chains, and pan traps of all sizes and scariness. One of them looked like an honest-to-God bear trap. Forge tongs, ice tongs, hay hooks, hay knives, hanging scales, lightning rod vanes that needed mending, and hardware store calendars from decades earlier decorated two of the walls. On another wall, above a cream separator with a broken handle, Grange meeting posters and product banners advertised events and tonics and liniments that were long gone before Don and I had been born. Possibly before my uncle had been born. The variety was endless. I had no idea what some items were. Don had a look of ever-increasing disbelief on his face. I was fascinated.

Frank, meanwhile, hunched over the tiny refrigerator, opened its locks and pulled out a half-gallon jug full of milk. Putting it directly to his mouth, he downed a good pint before handing it to us. Then he began unlocking the breadbox.

We looked around slowly, futilely, for a cup or glass of any kind. Realization dawned that there might not be any. I offered the jug to Don. "No way," he said quietly. "I don't care—I'm dying," I said, and tipped the jug to my mouth. Fresh, cold, sweet creamery milk never tasted so good.

Frank, seemingly energized by his duties as a host, had found an unopened box of almond windmill cookies, and offered us first pick. I took several and happily crunched away. I was hungry enough they tasted like a full-course meal. Don watched miserably, his mouth too dry for the cookies.

Frank and I passed the milk and cookies between us, feeling and looking visibly better with each mouthful. If he'd had a spare drop of moisture in him, Don would have drooled. The third time I offered him the milk, Don finally broke. His look said we weren't to tell his mother about this. But he had to agree, the milk and cookies were both fresh and first-rate.

"Byyy-yy-y God, boys, eat up and drink up," Frank said. "You've earned it."

By the time our ride home arrived, we both had $2.10 in pay and an invitation to come help again.

We went back several times that summer, me because I was fascinated by Frank's kitchen, and Don because he was being a good sport and keeping me company. Each time, we got seriously overworked and 35 cents an hour for our trouble. But we also got Frank's hospitality, freely and unstintingly offered.

We'd worked as hard as any men, we'd sweated under the same sun right along with him, and we were given the best of what he gave himself—the cold fresh milk and almond windmill cookies, in the kitchen, after the day's labor. ✳

133

Only One Life

BY CRAIG OSTREM

It is a cool crisp October afternoon and I am walking up a side-walk in a small southeastern Minnesota town. I see a plaque in the window of an antique store so I go inside. In the front window are old cooking utensils, a tin flour sifter, rolling pins, a large heavy mixing bowl and a plaque on the wall that reads, *"Only one life, that soon is past, only what's done with love will last"*. I immediately thought of Grandma Nelson, or Bertha to the folks in Lanesboro.

I remember Grandma Nelson best from when I was a child. She was vertically challenged, sturdy, with a steady demeanor. She wore felt-looking shoes that appeared to be a half size too small, with knee high pantyhose bunched around her ankles. Her slip hung, invariably, a half an inch below her cotton, floral, short-sleeve dress. And the aprons. She always wore an apron. She made many of her own clothes and I figured she must have sewn those aprons onto her dresses, until I saw her in church once without one. Grandma had dark gray hair the length of her height, and she wove it into a rope that she twirled around the top of her head into a bun. I used to look up at her imagining putting birdseed on top of her head and the sparrows lining the rim bobbing to an' fro. She wore black sturdy-rimmed glasses that framed a strong-featured face. A "grandma face" if ever there was one. She used to grab me to give me a hug and a kiss and her whiskers would tickle the nape of my neck until I laughed uncontrollably. Her appearance never changed all the years I knew her. She was always Grandma Nelson.

Grandma liked children. She would call the grandchildren into the house for a meal, stopping us at the front door to take off our shoes and roll down the cuffs of our pants onto discarded newspapers. There were coffee cans on both sides of the door, one side for marbles, rocks or sticks. The coffee cans on the other side had lids to restrain toads, baby birds and once a bat, but never snakes. Grandma didn't like snakes. She then marshaled us single file straight toward the kitchen sink where we stood on a sturdy white and red chair, washing our hands, stepping off the other side to the table for a scrumptious homemade meal. Grandpa liked meat and potatoes and of course there must be bread. We drank Specks nectar in different colored aluminum glasses that were cold to the touch and the tongue. There was generally a Jell-O salad, sometimes with marshmallows or chunks of pineapple. If we were lucky, dessert would be some of Grandma's white sugar cookies or pie made fresh from some fruit from Grandpa's garden. Afterward, we could help clear the table and Grandma would reach into the cupboard for a Mason jar full of change and press a nickel into the palm of our hands and instruct us to go to the Root Beer Stand to get some treats. A nickel would buy a large piece of taffy, Bazooka bubble gum and several Jolly Ranchers in those days.

One summer my cousins and I were out behind the garage in the rhubarb patch. We had taken our Boy Scout pocket knives and had cut the large rhubarb leaves into play money. The stalks made swords and spears. We even found some string to make bows and arrows. We were able to knock down apples with our spears to make piles that became enemy soldiers. Hours passed until we noticed a figure standing nearby. Looking up, pocket knives in hand, we noticed grandma standing there with her hands behind her back. As the tears began to roll down our faces she delivered an empty ice cream pail and placed it on the ground. After supper that night? You guessed it, rhubarb pie.

My childhood dream came true my junior year in high school as my father retired from the Air Force and bought a farm near that small, southeastern Minnesota town. For the rest of my high school days, I left school for lunch and crossed the street kitty-corner to greet my Grandpa on the porch and have a home cooked meal made by Grandma Nelson. Things were different then. Teenagers had something Grandma called "chores". "Idle hands are the devil's work", she would say. So there were weeds to pull, fruit and vegetables to pick, canning jars to bring up from the basement and canned goods to take down. There were storm windows to put on, take off, screens to replace and by golly it seemed like we painted the garage every other year. Grandma washed clothes in a barrel washer with rollers, and we used to haul the basket out to the clothesline where she would expertly hang all of the clothes and washed bedding to dry in the sun. Then we would haul the basket back into the house. If teenagers had chores, then Grandma had duties. I never saw her rest. Oh, she would occasionally play canasta or pinochle, but at the same time she was cooking a meal and holding a conversation, addressing envelopes for the church and writing down a grocery list.

Time marched on and I moved away from that small southeastern Minnesota town. I would visit Grandma occasionally. The house was always the same, the meals had become comfort food, and after a long visit Grandma would put some leftovers, slow cooked roast beef with potatoes and carrots into a Cool Whip container. If I was lucky she would put some white sugar cookies or pie wrapped in tin foil into the brown paper bag and I was off to challenge the world.

A few years later Grandpa passed away, and I remember Grandma looking regal in her funeral attire. After church we assembled at Grandma's house where we found comfort in the home cooked food and conversation. I was struck by how she comforted us, almost forgetting that she had lost her life-long companion. Time continued to pass and it was decided that Grandma should move to the nursing home in a nearby town. When visiting her there, she would greet me at the front door, arms outstretched, and then show me around the place. After our visit, she would pull a Mason jar from the bureau and she'd press a nickel into the palm of my hand and tell me to run up to the Root Beer Stand for a treat. I didn't have the heart to tell her that a nickel didn't buy much anymore, and the Root Beer Stand had since closed.

One Easter my mother, sister and I stopped in to visit Grandma. She didn't greet us at the front door as usual, so we headed down the long hall to her room. She was sitting in her wheelchair looking out the window at a large oak tree. We greeted her with smiles and hellos, but she didn't respond. She just kept looking out the window at that oak tree, its sturdy branches reaching towards heaven. As we left that morning, no one spoke. I guess we knew that, somehow, Grandma was no longer with us.

Only one life, that soon is passed, only what's done with love will last. ✳

Life's Lessons

Gary Fiene with a carp he probably hoped
to sell to Carl Johnson for fifty cents.

"Baseball and Red Horsin'"
PAGE 161

I have never let my schooling interfere with my education.

~ Mark Twain

Snoose

BY WAYNE PIKE

Wisdom always has a price, but it is gratifying to know that not every lesson in life has to be learned the hard way. Sometimes the other guy pays. That was the case when, as a boy, I learned the evils of "snoose", now commonly known as "smokeless tobacco".

It was a Saturday afternoon in the spring. Our neighbors, Ronny and Dale, called to ask if my three brothers and I could come up to their place to play ball. We were soon biking our way a mile to the east. Ronny, the star pitcher for our 4-H fast-pitch softball team, had an arm like a cannon. He was practicing with Dale when we rode in. When they saw us coming they dropped their gloves and motioned us to pull our bikes up to their old dairy barn. Obviously, they had something other than softball on their minds.

They led us into the barn and immediately got down on their knees in front of the cows. Digging through old ground corn and stale hay, they searched for something between the boards of the old wooden cow mangers. After a minute, they found a round tin can of Copenhagen chewing tobacco that they had stolen from their dad. Rather than hoard this prize, Dale and Ronny had decided to share it with us. We felt honored. We also felt scared of getting caught and excited at the prospect of this new, very adult, adventure.

Ronny opened the can and held it out flat in his palm. Dale, the oldest of our group, took the first pinch and placed it confidently in his mouth. Ronny quickly followed his older brother's lead. My brothers and I were a little slower. We studied Dale and Ronny who were being very careful not to let any signs of displeasure cross their faces. Making satisfied grunts and nodding our way, they urged us to take a pinch. They enticed us with a few very dry, modest spits.

My oldest brother, Richard, had already decided he was not going to join in. He made the same decision for our youngest brother, Mark. David, just two years older than I, and perhaps one of the most fastidious and hygienically correct human beings ever, leaned over the open tobacco can with me. He reached out as if to take a pinch, then paused and turned Ronny's outstretched hand toward the window to catch the light. David studied the dark material for a second and then calmly said, "Look. Worms."

Ronny and Dale both verified the finding during the next heartbeat. Sure enough, beneath a thin layer of tobacco were dozens of tiny white maggots. Then the spitting began in earnest. As the two chewers gagged, choked, and spat, Ronny wound up his rocket-launcher 4-H pitcher's arm and winged that old snoose can out the barn door into the manure pile. We got a good laugh and a good lesson. My brothers and I have had absolutely no desire for tobacco in any form after that. ※

Summer School (Psychology 101) on the Farm

By Elisabeth Olness Emerson

It was a glorious day in 1958 when the Blue Bird school bus, driven by Tyge Lee, took it's final trip for the school year. There was anticipation in the air for the last ride of the year from Peterson School to the end of my father's driveway, one mile east towards Rushford. Despite the fact I liked school and I had had a good fifth grade year, as I stepped off that large bus and said goodbye to my seat mate, Anne, I had a wonderful feeling of freedom. I walked from the bus to the house, my arms filled with notebooks and papers, the result of a year's work.

The summer, with all its possibilities, loomed ahead. I was looking forward to so many of the things that might happen. There were softball games with my three older sisters and brother, using the cow water tank as first base and the yard light pole as second. There might be a fishing trip with our neighbors, Odin and Bertha. On one hot day in June or July my mother would put on a pair of overalls, pack a lunch, and we would go to pick black-caps in the woods. We would return with red fingers and buckets of berries, and tales of seeing snakes. In July we would be haying. We hayed loose, and I would be needed to stomp it down in the hay rack. Later in the summer the oats and wheat were harvested, with my father driving the combine and myself helping to move the lever when the sack was filled with grain. I looked forward to bringing lunch to my father and brother while they worked in the fields, lying in the grass and talking with them while they ate. On

Sunday afternoons there would likely be get-togethers with relatives, my mother making another one of her delicious meals. My brother and I especially looked forward to the unusual summer visit from our city cousins, one of whom asked if the John Deere was a Buick. The summer promised trips to the gravel pit, to the Shell station for a pint of ice cream and red Kool Aid, to Winona for Krazy Days or Steamboat Days.

The possibilities for the summer seemed endless, and a number of them centered around my loyal playmates—the farm cats. I loved these cats, and gave each one a name which was carefully written in their medical records chart. The cats endured being weighed every once in awhile (for their medical records), and they obligingly wore some of my doll bonnets. I held them and petted them, and was always very sad when we lost one of them. Our farm was right next to Highway 16, and occasionally a cat would be lost while trying to cross the road. That would be followed by a funeral service, including burial in the cat cemetery which was right behind the granary. Each plot had a stone with the cat's name painted on it, and periodically I would plant flowers in this peaceful place.

It was my job to feed the cats twice a day, and I usually did this at the same times each day. The cats would start congregating around the back door of our house close to the time of feeding. In case I was a little late, their mewing reminded me. My mother kept a bowl of table scraps which were fed to the cats. Sometimes we added cooked oatmeal to this, and on fewer occasions we added store-bought cat food. This was distributed in several pans near the back door. Often I brought along a small pail of buttermilk as a treat. As I carried the food and milk from the house to the barn, I kept calling, "Here, kitty, kitty. Here, kitty, kitty." An entourage of farm cats-ran alongside of me, in front of me, in and out of my legs. I was the queen, and these cats were my court.

This was the period of life when I did a lot of imitating. When I went to a movie and saw an actor play the piano backwards, I figured out how to play "Long, Long Ago" while facing away from the piano, hands behind my back. When I observed a neighbor whistle for his dog, I wanted to do the same. Cats are just as smart as dogs, I thought. Could I teach them to come when I whistled? Years later, at the University of Minnesota, I would learn about operant conditioning in a psychology class. I couldn't even say "psychology" at this time in my life, but I intuitively had the concept of operant conditioning, and I developed a plan that I started the next day.

When it was feeding time for the cats, I stole out of the house, using a door opposite the side of the house where the cats gathered. I walked down to the barn, alone this time, with the food and milk. Once at the barn I started whistling. I could see the cats staring at the back door of the house, but none looked at me. I tried to whistle louder, and when there was no response I started walking toward the back door of the house where the cats were anxiously congregating. I kept whistling, and the cats looked at me, but they didn't seem to connect me with feeding time. Then one of them must have seen the food bucket and came to me. I interspersed my whistles with a few cries of "here, kitty, kitty" and soon I had the tribe moving with me down to the barn.

The next morning I did the same, carefully walking out of the door with the cats' food, going to the barn and whistling. For the first few days I would have to walk back towards the house to make sure all the cats were present for feeding time. The cats learned quickly, and soon I only had to give one short whistle, and there would be a thundering herd of cats racing to the barn for their breakfast or supper.

I felt so successful! I had trained cats to come when I whistled!

My success was not without problems, however. Yes, I had trained my cats to come when I whistled. I had also trained them, unwittingly, to come when *anyone* whistled. My father might be working on machinery and start whistling a tune. Suddenly, he would be surrounded by cats. The oil man might start whistling while he filled our tank. To his surprise, a dozen or more cats would suddenly appear tripping him as he moved about his work. My brother might whistle while he did chores, and he instantly had several furry helpers getting in his way.

Clamouring cats can be somewhat annoying when you are trying to work on machinery and have a lot of small parts spread around. After one unfortunate afternoon when my dad whistled while working on a delicate mechanical problem, he was overrun with cats, knocking his tray of small parts into the grass. He came into the house and said, "Lis, you have just got to get those cats to stop coming when anyone whistles."

It was actually getting a little annoying to me too, as I liked to whistle, so I decided I would stop whistling to the cats when I brought them their food. I stopped completely and went back to "here, kitty, kitty."

As I was to learn formally later at the University of Minnesota, however, it is not easy to unlearn this conditioned behavior. For weeks, months, even years, when anyone whistled on our farm, a cat or two might appear. I had done my operant conditioning well.

Of course, the cats weren't the only ones who were trained that summer. When any of us humans started to form our mouths for whistling, there was now a moment of hesitation. Did we really want a crowd of cats just then? Those clever farm cats had trained us, too. ✳

This story is dedicated to Old Susie, Susie, T-Bone, Smokey, Blackie, Norman, Muns, Buff, Marble, Nikita, Bootsin, Puff and several other dear cat friends from the 1950's and 1960's.

The Fort Snelling School Bus

By Curtis A. Fox

B efore I tell you about the school bus story I might mention that, as boys in our neighborhood, we seemed to get special pleasure in putting a penny on the railroad tracks, down near Minnehaha Park, so we could see how flat and squished it got from being run over. With a 74-year-old perspective on such boyhood incidents, it seems so innocent and boyish. It's just the way we were and maybe still are.

Reflecting as I do in writing this, a rather gentle smile is beginning to come over my heart and soul as I am reminded of the Fort Snelling school bus incident that took place when I was in the fourth grade at Minnehaha Elementary School. That would have made me right at nine years of age. My "boys will be boys" mentality must have suggested that it would be a great idea to put a can under the wheels of the school bus just to see how flat it would become. So, that is what I did. It took a little careful planning on my part. I saved and hid several "Carnation Evaporated Milk" cans so the can would have both ends intact in contrast with a can that had one end removed already. I even walked a whole block up to 51st Street and 46th Avenue to conduct this great can-flattening experiment. That was the corner where the bus always made its turn and in so doing came quite close to the corner itself. If you timed it just right you could toss the can so it would roll under rear wheels and get rather nicely crunched and flattened, giving you a fresh souvenir of your great and creative engineering skill.

It was a great idea, as long as it lasted, but sadly it was only for a day or two. Someone snitched on me and in very short order I was asked to report to the principal's office where I received a very stern lecture. As best I can recall, I was warned that the whole bus-load of kids might end up in the ditch and be killed just because I had thrown a can under the wheels of the bus.

I was put on probation, of sorts, and even got to be the "Teacher's Pet" by washing the blackboards and dusting the erasers after all of the other kids had been dismissed to go home. I had to stay after school until the school bus left in order to make sure my budding interest in flattened cans would not be enhanced by a schedule that might induce me to yield to the temptation. ✳

The Music Prodigy

By Margaret Boehmke

We were introduced to music at an early age in our farm home. It was the 1940's and there was no television at our house. Our radio connected us to the outside world. My mother played the radio station from Northfield, which included an all morning program of classical music. Paradoxically, my father enjoyed Country Western music and had an old radio perched on a shelf out in the barn. Although he didn't necessarily approve of this music for us girls, he played his barn radio full blast while milking the cows.

How they afforded it I do not know, but our parents made certain my sisters and I took piano lessons. I began in the second grade. I would sit at Miss Clara Reishus' piano, and she would count and tap out the timing for me—one and two and three and four. While in the first and second grades, we had what was called a rhythm band. This consisted of each of us clamoring with cymbals, castanets, sticks, bells, triangles, and drums. How we sounded I cannot imagine, but I must have absorbed an interest in music, for by the fourth grade I felt ready for a band instrument.

Some of my classmates, whom I admired greatly, played clarinets, and a clarinet was what I wanted. I begged and whined, and as luck would have it, my cousin had an old silver metal clarinet he wanted to get rid of. My parents purchased it for $40.00, and off I went for clarinet lessons, soon moving to the second band at Rushford Schools.

As I became more sophisticated, a metal clarinet simply wouldn't do—it proved to be something of an embarrassment. I wanted a black ebony clarinet, like my friends. Lo and behold, one Christmas I found one under the Christmas tree. Although it was 'used', I proudly carried my 'licorice stick' to school every day. By the seventh grade, I'd advanced to first band. Practicing wasn't a favorite pastime; I was now taking both piano and clarinet lessons. However, this did become a handy excuse to get out of dishes or other chores.

Being a member of the first band meant I was in concert, contests, quartets, and solos. It also meant getting to all the ballgames and area parades. One summer our band was invited to present an evening concert at the annual Steamboat Days festivities in Winona. Although most of the members rode to Winona by bus earlier in the day, I was given permission to ride in with my parents. My father finished his evening chores early, and our family headed to Winona, filled with excitement and anticipation.

A convenient parking place was nowhere to be found, so my father dropped me off as close as possible to the temporary, makeshift stage along the Mississippi River bank—the beautiful river was our backdrop. Already in my band uniform, I scurried on stage with my clarinet case in hand. The other band members were seated, and I hurriedly began to assemble my clarinet, when to my utter dismay I discovered I was minus a reed, that little piece of wood necessary to make music on a woodwind instrument! There was no time to borrow one from my friends, as their instrument cases were on the bus.

We were told that the boat regatta had begun on the Mississippi River behind us. Our director raised his wand and the music began, first a march, then a rhapsody. I knew my parents were somewhere in the audience, proudly stretching their necks to see their prodigy play. I fingered each note, faking the whole concert. The only sound coming forth was my breath!

Following the concert, we investigated the carnival, taking in every scintillating sound, smell, and taste. We indulged ourselves with hot dogs, pop, and ice cream bars, and much later watched the fireworks from a perfect spot. Only on the way home did I tell them about the clarinetist they really didn't hear, and we all had a good laugh.

Rapid changes have forced us to adjust to a more complicated way of life. These special times of long ago symbolize a time of parental involvement and pride. In the eyes of my parents, there was no doubt about it—I was their music prodigy. ✳

Sports Car Fever

By Jon Laging

When I was growing up, automobiles had an importance disproportionate to their actual role in our young lives. Of course, this was before computers, video games, or much TV. In our small town we would stand on the corner of the downtown park, eat from the popcorn wagon on band night, and tell each other the make and year of each car that drove past. There wasn't much else to do, except play catch, run errands for Mom and mow the lawn. Cars were easier to name in the "fifties." There were only three big automakers: G.M., Ford and Chrysler. There were other makes such as Hudson, Studebaker, Packard and Nash, but they weren't very common. Almost all were American except for a very rare Crosley.

The unusual cars were worth noting and if you saw one, you hollered at a friend to come see. The first compact car that we were aware of was the Henry J. It sold for less than a thousand dollars. All of us boys didn't think much of it. We thought it looked small and cheap. The public evidently agreed with us; before long the Henry J. disappeared. Our leanings were the other way. The bigger the better and there was no better car than the Cadillac. (Gosh, that guy must be rich!) Cars were part of growing up. You yearned to eventually get a driver's license. I think testosterone must be composed of car shaped molecules.

The first family car I drove was a 1941 Ford, the one with the high curved back end. We then traded for a 1951 Ford. There was nothing wrong with the '41. I think my mother got tired of it. The '51 had a "three on the tree" transmission and a powder blue and cream paint job. Pretty snappy.

Although I worked during the summer, the money was not spent on a car. It was for college. My father had left money for one year of college from his life insurance. My widowed mother accepted no alternatives. I went almost all the way through school with no car. I couldn't afford it. My senior year in college Mom gave me the '51 Ford. It was tired and had close to a hundred thousand miles on it. One of the older workers at my Mother's place of employment in Spring Valley offered to paint the Ford with a paint brush. Mom, thinking it could look no worse, agreed. She was wrong.

Given that I was twenty-two and had a paintbrush for a car, my car buying fever was running wild. When I got my first job in Rochester, I was ready. I bought car magazines including one on sports cars. My yearning had gone on so long it went in an unusual direction: sports cars. I looked at Jaguars. The Triumph TR3 looked interesting. Very rakish design, and a V in the front door allowed you to reach out and touch the pavement. I began my search. There were no Triumph dealers in Rochester, however, there was an MG dealer. I went and looked at MGs. I knew they had a red one available with wire wheels at $2,700. That was fairly close to a year's wages. I decided to give it a whirl, got in my paintbrush, and drove to Munger Imports.

Mr. Munger himself greeted me, not too unusual as he appeared to be the only salesman. The rest of the staff were mechanics. This should have been a tip off. I had read that Jaguar owners needed part time jobs just to pay for repairs. But of all the sports cars, MGAs were reputed to be the most reliable. In the future I would wonder about the accuracy of that statement.

Mr. Munger greeted me, casting a look at my paintbrush Ford parked a hundred feet away. The first question he asked was where I was working.

I told him, "The Rochester Methodist Hospital."

"Full time?"

"Yes, full time." He didn't exactly rub his hands together, but there was a gleam in his eyes.

The bank said OK and I became the proud owner of a streamlined beauty, a red MGA with wire wheels.

I entered the world of "bonnets", "boots," "windscreens" and "tyres." My stepdad and mom gave me a ride from Spring Valley to pick up the car. I signed off, put the top down and we got in my little red roadster. It was streamlined; in fact it sat only about two feet above the highway. On the way out of town I looked up as a semi passed me and was eye to eye with the undercarriage. I think Mom, my passenger, had a moment of doubt about my purchase.

The MGA was an unusual car, built with British sports car quirks. It had dual carburetors to give it additional horsepower. The 1600cc engine only developed 80 horsepower at 6000RPM. It had a tach, surprising in those days, but unless the carburetors were in tune, the car vibrated. I could stop at a red light and watch the radio antenna whip back and forth. There were two six-volt batteries connected in series, one on the left side of the car, the other on the right side to give balance as the car cornered.

Even given all the quirks, the car was a joy ninety percent of the time to drive and show off. The MG had very quick steering and it was important that you watched the road carefully. Particularly challenging was Highway 1 past Fugle's Mill on the way to Rochester. Along with the steering, the transmission, and four on the floor, the car kept you busy. Another interesting aspect of the convertible was that if it was raining, you could still keep dry if it was driven at a high speed.

Sports cars were seldom seen back then and I scared the devil out of my friends with its tight cornering. The best way to do this was to head into a left turn at an intersection, shift into second and increase the speed. This was particularly effective if there was a car coming the other way. The brave passenger would grab the armrest, and freeze. The nervous might scream softly.

The car for all its looks did not have much acceleration. Young guys with their Detroit Iron often wanted to drag me. Whenever I was in an especially good mood, and if the opposing driver had his girlfriend in the car, I would oblige. The MG and I would really try, but we would always get beat. I watched them go ahead with the proud driver looking at his girlfriend.

The car was a great deal of fun and I don't know if it was the reason I met my wife, but I have always wondered. Both Kay and I really enjoyed the MG until she became pregnant and the little car wasn't practical. I sold it and welcomed another adventure in my life: twin sons. ✺

Guilty

By Richard Holle

He was thirteen in that autumn of 1947. The air was crisp with the fall colors in full splendor. Saturday usually was the day the lad would take his old .22 rifle, call his dog, Jiggs, and disappear for the day into the woods on Maggelson Bluff squirrel hunting.

This day was different. The watermelons on the Brunner farm just north of Rush Creek were ripe. It was the custom for the Brunner brothers to back their old flatbed truck to the melon patch, load it and drive to the parking lot at the cemetery and sell their produce. The boy and three of his pals knew the drill and made the plan for the raid. They waited below the bank of the creek, watching the two men load the truck and head toward town

The boy knew it was wrong. "Thou Shalt Not Steal" rang in his ears. He was insecure and did not want to seem weak in the eyes of his friends. The truck rolled away. There was a mad scramble into the patch. Each grabbed a melon and ran halfway up the nearby bluff. Totally out of breath, they collapsed as a group and eyed their booty. One by one they cracked a melon and full face plunged into the red flesh.

Next morning, Sunday, the alarm woke the lad. He arose, sponged off as there was no shower or bath, dressed and headed for church. That morning, Mrs. Otterstad, the minister's wife, was making "assignments" in Sunday school. "You will be a missionary in Madagascar." Then it was out and around to the side door of the magnificent stone Rushford Lutheran Church. Once inside, he and his friend could hear the organ beginning to drone the call to the faithful, and had to scramble into the proper vestments to light the candles for the service. Then, they ran outside, in the front, and up the stairs in time to sing in the choir. Throughout the whole exercise, the boy struggled with guilt. "Hypocrite" was not a word in his vocabulary, but that was the overwhelming feeling.

After church, he walked the short block home, had a bite to eat, and then mounted the good old Radio Flyer to gather the Sunday Tribune for delivery. In the night, the bundle of papers was dropped on the corner in front of Jaastad's Hardware. The wire that wrapped the papers was tight and hard and required pliers to free the pack. He had gained independence at that time. It was agreed that he would pay $.25 of the weekly newspaper wage of $1.25 for room and board. He never revealed the raid on the watermelons at home.

The last paper on the Sunday route was the only paper in North Rushford. It was the minister's paper. There was a walking bridge across Rush Creek, near the mill to the other side of Rush Creek near the parsonage. He was cold and tired and did not see that someone had removed the board cover on the approach to the bridge. He pumped faster up the grade. Crash! Upsidedown! The last Sunday paper everywhere! Pain. Everything hurt. Gathering papers, he hoped nobody was looking. Duty bound, he delivered Reverend Otterstad's Sunday paper. When he was finally home, the telephone rang.

"Hello? This is Mr. Otterstad. We are missing section five of the Sunday paper."

"Umm... I will be there in five minutes."

He found the section five in his home paper. He was sure God was looking. God had been looking when he bit the melon.

The following Saturday, he waited until the melon truck went to town. On the shabby little house beside the melon patch, there was a front porch with a Ball or Mason canning jar on the corner. He dropped a quarter in the jar. It was half full of a clear liquid. Rumor was the brothers made bathtub gin. He watched it sink to the bottom and then ran to the creek bank. He did not want to be seen, though he knew it was the right thing. ✳

157

My First Cigarette

MARY JO DATHE

If I'd known then what I know now, my story might have been different. I was about thirteen years old, a freshman in high school, and smoking was almost unheard of among "nice" kids.

But let's back up a bit. In 1944, when World War II was raging, the government was getting very short on manpower and my Dad was drafted into the army. It seemed so unfair—he was 32 years old, a father of four, and working a small farm north of Spring Valley. However, no excuses were valid from healthy males, so off he went. Mom moved us to Racine near her relatives, and within a year the war was over. Dad came home a confirmed smoker, the first time I was really in contact with someone who smoked cigarettes.

In my close-knit group of friends, none smoked. Even in our class of forty-some students, no one smoked openly. Maybe "behind the barn" or on a date, but definitely not in public. Perhaps there were good reasons. It just wasn't the thing to do as smoking was more an adult thing. Money was hard to come by. We girls would rather spend our hard-earned baby-sitting dollars on better things. Like what? Like nylon stockings (remember the garter belts and crooked seams?) or permanent wave kits to curl our hair, or Avon's newest fragrances, my favorite being Topaz.

Anyway, on to my first cigarette. A girl I'll call DeeDee that I had gone to school with in Spring Valley invited me to come for an overnight visit. Our folks were still "going back and forth" to Spring Valley and my Dad worked the night shift at the local creamery, so it worked out well for my ride to town. DeeDee and I had supper with her folks and then she suggested we go downtown to the bowling alley to check out the scene. Despite the aforesaid nightspot being where the "wild" boys hung out, I was game, as we might see kids I'd gone to school with years before.

We left her house, hiked through the darkened park on the school grounds, and away from prying eyes she pulled out a pack of cigarettes and offered me one. How could I say no? I was about to embark on what is termed a learning experience. She lit up her cigarette, took a drag, and blew out smoke like a pro. Being a neophyte, I did just what she did, and then...nearly died. I choked, coughed, gasped, tears streamed down my cheeks, and I struggled to catch my breath. When I finally could breathe again and regain my voice, I managed to sputter that I guessed I was not ready for this, and would just as soon pass. The rest of the evening wasn't that much fun either, and sorry to say, it cast a pall on our friendship, and I did not stay over again. However, I will always be grateful to DeeDee. It was not only my first cigarette, it was also my last, as I was never again tempted to try to smoke.

Nicotine must be a terrible addiction. These days we see lovely young women outside public buildings where smoking is banned, cigarettes in hand, sucking those poisons into their systems. Or a young mother driving along, a cigarette in one hand on the wheel, a cell phone in the other, often with a child strapped into a carseat, subjected to those lethal fumes. I want so much to show them two pictures I carry of my dear sister. At age twenty-four, Barb was working as a beautician, a beautiful woman with sparkling blue eyes, clear complexion, and gorgeous wavy brown hair but already a chain smoker. Twenty-five years later she was dying of smoking-related cancer. After eight years of surgeries, chemotherapies and radiation, she had no hair, her ravished body was covered with scars and sores, and cancer had invaded multiple organs, bones, and her brain. I held her hand when she died at the care center at the age of forty-nine.

A good friend is today dying from the same battle with those "cancer sticks." She, too, was a popular, talented beauty but now her wasted body needs a wheelchair for mobility and she is on oxygen around the clock, a shadow of her former self. And do you know what she tells me? "If I had known what I know today, I'd never have taken that first cigarette." ❋

Baseball and Red Horsin'

By Gary Feine

The neighborhood of Jerusalem in the city of Rushford still brings back many fond childhood memories, most of them connected to fishing the "Mighty Root" and baseball.

For boys growing up in Rushford during the 50's and 60's, baseball was a major part of life. Three people in particular come to mind as major promoters, namely Ben Niggle, Rees Johnson and Walt Britt. Nobody treated the baseball kids better than "Mr. Baseball" Ben. I still remember Rees passing the hat for donations during the city team baseball games and Walt has to be considered the Satchell Paige of Rushford. Those guys even paid a nickel for any foul ball retrieved by one of us kids.

When we weren't playing baseball, or watching it, we were listening to it while we fished. Fishing was automatic in our neighborhood, especially in the spring when the "Red Horse" started running. Our neighborhood was right at the confluence of Rush Creek and the Root River. School did not get out fast enough and weekends were not long enough when the Red Horse were hot. It was not uncommon for us to fill gunny sacks full of fish caught on night crawlers or angle worms.

There was no limit on Red Horse since they are considered rough fish. Sometimes we would clean them and sell them throughout the neighborhood. Once in awhile, my grandpa, Ed Peterson, would take them and occasionally Manion's hogs received an extra treat for the day. I remember we had a price list for the different species of fish caught. Red Horse were whatever we could get for them. Trout, when they were in season, were 50 cents apiece, and once in awhile, if Carl Johnson wanted a carp to smoke, he would give us 25 cents for one.

One day we had an enormous carp and took it to Carl. He said that he would take it for the usual "two bits." But this was a big one, and we tried to work him for "four bits." Carl, in his bartering strategy to get it for 25 cents, said that if he paid 50 cents he would have to report our business to Sheriff Haugerud to make sure everything was legal, that we were reporting our income and paying taxes. We assured him that was no problem, as all we wanted was the 50 cents. We were also well aware that Carl was a pretty good B.S.er, and that there was just one sheriff and one deputy in Fillmore County, and our odds of avoiding them were pretty good. We decided to take our chances and laughed all the way to the store to spend our money on baseball cards and candy.

The next morning, while walking home from the baseball field, sure as heck Sheriff Haugerud was cruising the streets of Rushford. I'm sure he was not looking for two kids who sold a carp for 50 cents, but of course we didn't know that, and Carl bought his carp from then on for two bits. ✳

Biographies

Carol Hahn Schmidt's senior picture, 1931

"Senior Banquet"
PAGE 94

"The Wheelchair Ride"
PAGE 97

*A man travels the world over in search of
what he needs, and returns home to find it.*

~George Moore

Jo Anne Agrimson lives with her husband, Keith, on their farm in Arendahl Township. Aside from writing, she spends most of her time teaching language arts and making plans to visit the couple's two children, Stephanie and Jacob, college students in the Twin Cities.

Ida Mae I. Bacon moved to Fillmore County about six years ago and feels she has lived here her whole life. She is married, has four children (Tim in New Carlise, Indiana; Aaron in Lombard, IL; Kelvin in Lannon, WI; and Angi in Winona, MN) seventeen grand children, and four great grand children with the fifth due at the end of October. She works with the Rushford Children's Reading Theater and dabbled in drama this last summer. She likes to write poetry and short stories when she feels a tug about events or particular objects.

Steve Befort grew up in Fountain and is a 1966 graduate of Preston-Fountain High School. After practicing law for eight years, he joined the University of Minnesota Law School faculty where he has taught since 1982. He now lives in St. Paul with his wife Anne Johnson and his daughters, Anna and Grace.

Margaret Boehmke was raised on a dairy farm west of Rushford, and attended Rushford Public Schools. However, most of her adult years were spent living in Michigan, where she was employed by the Michigan House of Representatives. Upon retirement in 2002, she could no longer resist the urge to return to her Scandinavian roots, and now resides in Rushford. Her secret passion is writing, and she has three grown children plus two grandchildren. She says she will never tire of the beautiful hills and valleys of SE Minnesota.

Rose Breitsprecher was raised on a farm in Norway Township, attended the Maland country school, and graduated from Peterson High School. She farms with her husband, Alan, south of Canton, across the border in Iowa. They have two daughters and four grand-children: Colin, Olivia, Anastasia, and Katharina. She enjoys quilting, knitting, gardening and reading.

As a youngster, **John Brink** spent a lot of time on both his grandparents' farms by Granger and Henrytown. He went to school in Harmony. He and his wife, Tammy, have three daughters and one granddaughter. He works on an Angus farm in the Mabel-Canton area.

Artist **Charles Capek** spent his childhood school years in Rochester and many summers with his Mulhern cousins on their Fountain farm. He calls Fillmore County "a paradise for artists and for anyone who appreciates the character and generational memories that exist in a particular land and its people and animals."

Beverly Lewis Crowson and husband Vern live in the Chatfield area where they were raised. They have two children and seven grandchildren. She taught junior high language arts in Hayfield, Preston, and Chatfield, the latter for twenty-two years. She values time for family, friends, snowbirding, reading, writing, and dancing. She loves playing with Chatfield Lutheran's Handbell Choir and working in Lanesboro at Olivia's Attic.

Mary Jo (Boucsein) Dathe has always lived in Fillmore County, married fifty years to Gordon Dathe. Her hobbies include volunteering at the Spring Valley Historical Society, photography, birding, reading, and family history scrapbooks. She is writing her life story for her grand-daughters, Rheanna, Kristen, Alicia and Rosalyn.

Tom Driscoll, a Rushford resident, studied at the Iowa Writer's Workshop. He served in the Army, Peace Corps and USAID. His work has appeared in literary magazines, *Wisconsin Architect, City Lights* (Madison) and *The Fillmore County Journal*. Bleu a volume of selected poems, was published by Rocket Science Press in 1997.

Elisabeth Emerson grew up on a farm near Peterson, Minnesota, and graduated from Peterson High School in 1965. She has had a career in the field of public health and currently works for the World Health Organization in Thailand. Elisabeth is married to Al Emerson, and they have two daughters and three grandsons.

Gary Feine was born and raised in the Rushford area. He graduated from St. Charles High School and earned his bachelors degree from Winona State University. He began teaching in the Preston school system in 1976 and remains within the Fillmore Central School system. Gary resides in Preston with his wife, Kate, and is the proud father of Lucas and Caleb.

Curtis Fox is a retired Lutheran Pastor living in the old "Boyum Home Place" near Peterson where his wife Doris grew up. He was ordained for the ministry at Arendahl Lutheran Church in 1957. He continues in active pastoring as an "Interim", having been recently at Fountain and Root Prairie Lutheran in Fillmore County.

Dana Gardner was raised in Lanesboro, and now makes his home in Berkeley, California. A free-lance illustrator, he returns to Lanesboro frequently to collaborate with Nancy Overcott on books and articles about the birds and natural history of southeastern Minnesota and the Midwest.

Timothy M. Gossman was raised on a family farm in Freedom Township in Waseca County, Minnesota. He is a graduate of Waldorf-Pemberton High School and St. John's University. He has been a farm loan officer at Root River State Bank since 1986 and is involved with several environmental and community organizations. He and his wife, Susan, live on their farm in Jordan Township, Fillmore County, with their daughters, Sophia and Sarah. The family raises Christmas trees, forest trees, honey bees and a few head of livestock. Tim also enjoys family vacations, gardening, canning, barbecuing, native plants and running.

A lifelong resident of the Cherry Grove area, **Bonnie Heusinkveld** and her husband Cleon now live on an acreage where they can view the dairy farm where she was born and raised. They have two sons who now operate the farm with a grandson. Her hobbies include bowling, flower gardening and great grandchildren.

Herb Highum is a lifelong resident of Fillmore County. He farmed on a Century farm (1873) in Arendahl township from 1961-1999. He has also been an assistant at Hoff's Funeral Homes for twenty years. He enjoys singing and is very active in church and civic affairs. He's served on the Winona Community Hospital board, and the Zoning and Planning Commission in Rushford. Herb married Ruby Tweten in 1952. They have three children, seven grandchildren, and two great grandchildren.

Richard Holle was born at 411 E. Grove St. in Rushford. His education began with kindergarten in Whalen, then twelve years in Rushford schools. From there he earned a B.A. and M.S. at Winona State University, studied biology and psychology at U.C.L.A., was a graduate of Chinese-Mandarin from the Army Language Institute, received a National Science Foundation grant from U.C. Berkley in geology/paleontology and another N.S.F. grant from Yale University. He served the U.S. Army Security Agency in the Far East, and taught biology for nineteen years in Los Angeles. He invested in real estate and says he was "lucky, but my best fortune is my wife—the love of my life for fifty years."

Signe (Aasum) Housker has been a resident of Fillmore County for 77 years. She attended Riceford rural school (in Houston County) and Mabel High School, graduating in 1946. After several years of employment at a Rochester hospital, she married Bernard Housker. They farmed in Preble Township and had two children, Robert on the home farm and Carol Christensen, Ft. Collins, Colorado. After becoming a widow, Signe resides in Mabel.

Jeff Kamm is a Lanesboro resident. He is a passionate birder and trout fisherman. Jeff fell in love with Lanesboro and Fillmore County the first time he tossed a spinner in the Root River.

Jon Laging's early years and MGA adventures took place in Spring Valley. He worked at the Rochester Methodist Hospital, then as a Hospital Personnel Director in Sioux Falls, South Dakota, and Salina, Kansas. He lives in Preston, writes a sports column, and is a Seasonal DNR Naturalist. Jon's a husband, father and grandfather.

Ann Lemke was born and raised in Spring Valley and is a sixth generation Fillmore County resident on her mother's side, third generation on her father's. She received a BA in English from Winona State University and works in medical publications. After several years away, she now enjoys home ownership back in Spring Valley.

Mary Lewis lived on a nut farm near Amherst from 1975-1994, with her husband and two sons. Devoted to sustainable agriculture through the cultivation of nut crops such as hazels, Badgersett Farm continues without her now. Presently she lives in Decorah, Iowa where she teaches biology at Luther College, and works at developing her writing.

Al Mathison is a Preston area farmer and truckdriver. He is the author of "Images of America: Preston" published by Arcadia Press in 2004. Perhaps someday he'll write another book.

Born and raised on a dairy farm west of the cities (Wayzata) **Kathleen Schommer Mulhern** graduated from St. Mary's School of Nursing, Rochester. She exchanged her starched cap for an apron to raise her six children on a dairy farm near Wykoff. Now retired, volunteer work for church and community and various hobbies keep her busy.

Anna Rae Nelson grew up in Fillmore County near Peterson. She really learned to appreciate the area while away for five years at college in River Falls, Wisconsin. She now resides right near her "childhood stomping grounds" with her husband and two daughters where she raises and trains horses full time.

Wallace Osland grew up on a farm in the Greenleafton area of Fillmore County. Following completion of a Mortuary Science degree in 1965, he and his wife moved to Spring Valley where they raised two daughters and operated the Osland Funeral Home and Osland Ambulance Service. Wallace and Ann retired in 1996 and now enjoy living in their log home in rural Lanesboro.

Craig Ostrem is a 1975 graduate of Lanesboro High School, and a 1979 graduate of the U of M. He resides in Edina, Minnesota, with his wife Linda and two sons: James (10) and Charlie (8). He is a partner and the VP of Investments for Van Clemens & Co., a brokerage firm, in downtown Minneapolis. Forays to the family farm continue to be a welcomed respite from city life. Craig and his sons get their hair cut in Fillmore County at Leon's Barbershop in Harmony, where Craig has been a customer for over thirty years. His parents, Jim and Ruth Ostrem, still reside on the farm just outside of Lanesboro. His aunt Margaret Nelson lives in the house of Craig's grandparents, Bertha and Bill Nelson, and it is still a familiar place to congregate.

Nancy Overcott lives with her husband and cats in the Big Woods south of Lanesboro. She is a columnist for *The Fillmore County Journal* and *Minnesota Birding*. She indulges her love of wild birds in morning walks and in the writing of two new books, with illustrator Dana Gardner, forthcoming from the University of Iowa Press.

La Verne Paulson was raised on the original Eide farm on North Prairie. He spent twelve years in the Peterson Schools, then graduated from Winona State College with a degree in elementary education. After teaching thirty-five years in Preston, he retired in 2003.

La Verne still lives in Preston with Denise, his bride of thirty years. They have two sons, Erik and Brett.

Erik Paulson is the eldest son of LaVerne and Denise Paulson. He was born in Spring Valley in 1976 and grew up in Preston. Erik attended college at three different institutions: Winona State, Minnesota State University – Akita, Japan, and UW-Milwaukee. He holds a BA in History.

Wayne Pike was raised on a farm near Rochester, Minnesota. He attended a one-room country school and, eventually, the University of Minnesota. He has been a dairy farmer and a farm management instructor for Riverland Community College. Wayne is a student of rural life and writes about that in his column, *Township Roads*, which has appeared in the *Fillmore County Journal* since 1997. Besides writing, Wayne enjoys reading, public speaking and fixing things. He lives on his home farm with his wife, Deb. Bob, Matt and Ted are their three children.

Rich Prinsen was born and raised in York township near Greenleafton, on a family farm that he and his wife Joyce have made home for their entire married life, nearly fifty years. They have four children and seven grandchildren. Richard's story "A Teacher, a Rooster, and an Outhouse" inspired the title for the first Story Project book in 2003.

Donovan "Don" Ruesink is a retired, lifetime farmer in the Cherry Grove area. He attended grade school at Cherry Grove and is a Wykoff High School graduate. He has served on several area boards, and is currently a Forestville Township supervisor. His father is the merchant that inspired his story "Village Lottery."

Carol Hahn Schmidt grew up in rural Preston. After graduating in 1931, she took her Normal Training there and taught school in Dutch Hollow School for three years. She and her husband, Gerald, farmed in Carimona, where they raised three sons. In 1967 they moved to Rochester and at the age of 60, she earned her B.S. degree at Winona State in Elementary Education. She taught at St. John's Parochial School for ten years. In 1979 they returned to Preston to live. Carol died Oct. 19, 2004, at the age of 91.

Tracy Schommer is a Franciscan Sister of Little Falls, Minnesota. She has been a teacher all of her life, having taught all levels from elementary to college. She has retired from teaching and now enjoys dabbling in many of her other interests: writing, working with the elderly and youth. She enjoys nature, music, and travel, and now resides in Preston with her four-legged friend, Rosemary. She is an aunt to Charles Capek, artist and writer, and a sister to Kathy Mulhern who also has a story in this book.

Cheryl Hendrickson Serfling is a fourth generation Fillmore County resident who attended country school at "Empire" near Cherry Grove and high school at Wykoff. She and her husband farm near Greenleafton, have three grown children and two grandchildren, and think country living is always an adventure.

Marcella Shipton was born on a farm in Fillmore County. She graduated from Wykoff High School in 1943, and got married in 1947. After farming for most of their married lives, she and her husband are now retired and still live on the farm on County Road 14, on top of Rifle Hill, in a frame house with their beautiful collie dog, Babe.

Marjorie Smith has lived in Rushford since 1958. Her education was obtained at Clyde (country) School, St. Charles High, Bemidji State University, and Winona State University. She taught fourth grade for many years in Rushford. Retirement for her husband of fifty-nine years and Mrs. Smith allows them to enjoy their one daughter and two grandsons. Gardening and travel, in addition to reading about it, fill the time remaining.

Peter Snyder's ties to Fillmore County are parents, grandparents, and great grandparents who were all born and raised here. The Elliott ancestral farm south of Harmony is nearing 150 years of continual Elliott family ownership. The Snyder family started and owned for years what is now the Pine Tree Apple Orchard. Peter went to St. Charles schools but lived on the Winona County /Fillmore County line south of St. Charles/Utica. He now resides north of Lanesboro in an area referred to as "the prairie".

Marjorie Evenson Spelhaug was born in Whalan in the same house in which her dad was born. Her parents were Adolph and Elva Sorum Evenson. She attended grade school in Whalan and graduated from Lanesboro High School. She attended Winona State Teachers College for one year, taught rural school for two years, and was a bookkeeper for several years. She married Vernon Spelhaug and moved to Fountain. They had two children, Kathy and Mark. She retired in 1995 from the First State Bank of Fountain after twenty years of employment there.

Gary Stennes was raised and still lives in Rushford. He graduated from Rushford High School in 1989 and now works at Boelter Industries in Winona. He married his wife Kristi in 2000 and they have three children: Sawyer, Madeline and Jacob.

After growing up in Idaho and spending summers on her grandpa's farm north of Peterson, **Becky Stocker** is finally able to call that farm her home. She moved here in the fall of 2004 and fills most of her time as a wife and mom. Living in a rural area for the first time in her life, Becky is still constantly "wowed" by the beauty of Fillmore County, especially all the stars she can see at night.

P.J. (Pamela Jean) Thompson was born in Colorado and moved to the City of Rushford Village in February of 2002. She is a wife, a mother and grandmother who finds a song or a story in the scenery and people of the area. She is the current Chancellor of the Catholic Diocese of Winona who enjoys writing, photography, painting and playing music in her leisure time.

Carol Thouin grew up and graduated from high school in Spring Valley. She earned degrees in Speech Communications and Journalism from St. Cloud State University, married and eventually moved back "home" to Spring Valley to raise two sons. She's currently Director of Marketing Communications for Home Federal in Rochester.

John Torgrimson is the editor of the *Fillmore County Journal*, a weekly newspaper in Preston, Minnesota, that he owns with his wife Pat. Before taking over the *Journal* in 1996, John spent more than 20 years working in human services, much of it abroad. He has lived and worked in the Solomon Islands in the South Pacific, the Philippines and Hong Kong. He and his wife have two children, Neale and Emily, and live on a small farm near Preston.